"This to
is like family."

Cassie followed Dan to a table in the crowded restaurant. "I'm not saying that's *all* good," she added. "There's a negative side, too."

"For instance?" Dan asked.

"You may not have noticed, but at least fifteen people watched us cross the room. Some of them are looking at us right now." Cassie lowered her voice. "And some of them are thinking things."

"What kind of things?"

"My guess is that about half of them are laying odds that you'll never get anywhere with me. The other half's decided that we're already an item. They can hardly wait for tomorrow so they can spread the word to the people who weren't here tonight."

Dan gazed at Cassie. He was almost afraid to ask, but he was burning to hear what she'd say. "Which half is right?"

"The first half, of course," she replied lightly.

Dan's voice deepened as he challenged her. "I wouldn't be so sure of that, Cassie...."

Karen Percy is one talented lady! Not only is she a romance writer, she's also a gifted musician. Her career as a percussionist for the Los Angeles Philharmonic actually began in a small California town similar to Pinetop. During her childhood, she attended summer music camp just outside the town, and later returned as a faculty member. Karen continues to bring her dual talents to the classroom, teaching both writing and percussion at the University of California. *The Home Stretch* is Karen's first Temptation.

The Home Stretch

KAREN PERCY

Harlequin Books

TORONTO • NEW YORK • LONDON
AMSTERDAM • PARIS • SYDNEY • HAMBURG
STOCKHOLM • ATHENS • TOKYO • MILAN

FORTY YEARS OF
Romance

Published July 1989

ISBN 0-373-25360-5

1

CASSIE MCLEAN eyed the pool table and concentrated on her shot. "Four ball in the corner pocket," she announced.

Her opponent was a lean, blond young man who wore his cowboy hat perched at a rakish angle. "You'll never make it, McLean."

"What do you want to bet, Webley?"

Jack Webley delved into a jeans pocket and pulled out a dollar bill. "This says you don't have a prayer."

"You're on." Cassie bent over the table to position herself for the difficult shot. From the corner of her eye, she could see Jack moving around behind her. She felt, rather than saw, his hand moving closer to her rounded, jean-covered derriere.

She said mildly, "Try it, Webley, and you'll pull back a stump."

Jack's hand, thumb and forefinger poised for a pinch, froze in midair. "Dang it, Cassie! How did you know? You got eyes in the back of your head or somethin'?"

Cassie shook her head, her short, golden-brown hair lifting then subsiding like flower petals tossed by a playful breeze. "I just know you, Jack. I know all your sneaky little tricks." She had known Jack, and almost everyone else in Pinetop, her entire life. There were never many newcomers to the small, Southern California mountain town—except for tourists, who didn't count, and summer people, whose cabins were empty most of the year, and who didn't count, either.

A goodly number of Pinetoppers—the real thing, the year-round residents—were gathered for a Saturday night out at the Pinetop Pizza Bar. Now that it was October, there weren't many temporaries around anyway, and those who did appear in town—at the bakery, the grocery store, the gift shops and the two fancy restaurants—seemed to understand instinctively that the Pizza Bar was reserved for locals.

Jack had the good grace to look sheepish. "It's just . . . aw, I don't know. You got such a cute little bottom, a man can't help wantin' to . . ."

"I'll thank you to keep your eyes to yourself, Jack Webley, as well as your hands. Now are you going to let me make my shot?"

"Why, sure. Go right ahead."

Cassie made certain he had stepped back, out of pinching range, before she again leaned over the table. The shot required all her concentration. She was temporarily oblivious to the smells of pizza and cigarette smoke, the country-Western singer lamenting from the jukebox and the hum of many simultaneous conversations going on in the big room adjacent to the alcove where the pool tables were located.

She tapped the cue ball. It whizzed down the table and struck the six ball, which gently tapped brown number four. Number four teetered on the edge of the pocket, then, almost reluctantly, rolled in.

"All *right!*" she said triumphantly as she straightened. "Pay up, Webley." But Jack's gaze was focused on the main part of the room. "Hey, you weren't even watching!"

"Huh? Oh, sorry, Cassie." Jack looked back at the table. "Okay, here's the buck I owe you."

He handed over the dollar bill, but his gaze instantly drifted back to something that was going on near the bar, a small eddy of activity amid the other eddies in the big open-beamed room.

"What's so fascinating over there?" Cassie asked.

"It's the new doc."

"New doc?"

"Yeah, the tall guy. See?"

Cassie followed the direction of Jack's gaze. A tall figure, his back turned, stood in a little group, which included Cassie's best friend, Mary Jo Cooper. All at once, she understood Jack's interest. He'd been crazy about Mary Jo since the sixth grade. In the ten years since high school, Jack and Mary Jo had dated each other from time to time, then broken up for a variety of reasons. But now, their relationship was "on" again, and the whole town was watching to see whether, this time, it would last.

Then the tall man turned, answering some remark or other, and his eyes happened to meet Cassie's. For an instant their gazes locked and held. Then someone spoke to him and he turned away again . . . leaving Cassie with no breath in her body.

That's him!

The words seemed to appear in her mind, not as if she had thought them, but as if some force outside herself was responsible. But there was no question what they meant. *That's him!* The man for her. The one she hadn't even known she was waiting for.

The next instant she blinked, cursing herself for a fool. She must be crazy, thinking something so damned dumb. But the man *was* attractively strong-featured, with an assertive nose and masculine jaw. His dark hair grew a little long over his collar, as if he hadn't had time for a haircut recently. And that moment when he'd looked at her, he had an expression in his eyes that Cassie found undecipherable. But to think such thoughts about some tourist . . .

Only he wasn't a tourist, was he?

She turned to Jack, who was still wistfully regarding Mary Jo. "Doctor? I didn't know Pinetop was getting a new doctor. I wouldn't think there'd be enough business for another one."

Jack looked astonished. "Where's your brains, McLean? He's the new vet. You, of all people, ought to know that."

Jack had a point. Like everyone else in town, she knew that Doc Anderson—the kindly, white-haired man she had learned to rely on when one of her horses was ill or injured—could no longer take the harsh winters on the mountain. He had found a temporary replacement to carry on the practice until he could sell it. She had already heard, via Pinetop's efficient jungle drums, that the replacement had arrived in town today.

"Oh, right," she said slowly. "I guess I just forgot."

Jack regarded the group surrounding the new vet, which still included Mary Jo. "Hey, McLean, don't you think we ought to go over and introduce ourselves? Make the new doc feel welcome and all?"

Cassie shook her head, unprepared for a closer encounter with the man who'd had such a strong effect on her from a distance. "You go, Jack. I think I'll stay here."

Jack gave her an odd look. "What's got into you, McLean? You're usually the most sociable one in the bunch."

She waved her cue. "I want to practice a couple of shots...so I can trounce you even more thoroughly than usual."

"Well, okay. I'll be back in a minute."

Cassie bent over the pool table. She set up an easy shot...and missed. Another, even easier one, also went awry. *Drat!* Coming all unglued over some man, some stranger, wasn't like her. She had thought her defenses well fortified and perfectly emplaced. Of course, it had been years since there had been any real test of the ramparts. She had known all of Pinetop's eligible males since she was in diapers and, although she had many friends among them, not a single masculine Pinetopper had ever elevated her temperature by so much as a single degree.

Looks like that's about to change, McLean, she told herself ironically. Unless that fleeting moment was pure illusion—which she hoped desperately would prove to be the case—it was going to be a tough winter. Or a tough couple of months, anyway. No one knew how long the new vet was going to stay in town. It all depended on how long it took Doc Anderson to sell his practice.

What *was* known, however, was that the new vet's stay in Pinetop was only temporary. Which meant that, as far as Cassie McLean was concerned, he was unavailable . . . as off limits as if he were married and the father of six.

She hadn't a prayer of successfully avoiding him, though. Even if Pinetop weren't so small that you saw practically everybody every day, she was bound to have to call him sooner or later. What was she supposed to say to a sick horse? *Sorry, Flame.* Or Banjo. Or Star. *You'll just have to weather it on your own. I can't call the vet because seeing him does funny things to my insides.*

She snorted contemptuously at herself as she leaned over to make another easy shot . . . which she also missed.

This was ridiculous!

She took a sip of the beer she had been nursing all evening, then reracked the balls. Summoning all her concentration, she bent over the table and poised for the break.

"Could you use some competition?" a deep voice said from behind her.

Cassie jumped. Her cue jerked and struck the cue ball, which did a merry little hop and landed with an embarrassing thud on the green felt. The rest of the balls were untouched, still bunched in their original triangle.

She whirled, ready to glare at the person who had startled her, and found herself facing a broad chest and sturdy shoulders, covered by a plaid, long-sleeved shirt. The sleeves were rolled up to bare muscular forearms.

It was him. She might have known it would be him, the *him* she least wanted to find in close proximity to herself. Unfortunately he looked even better than he had at a distance. His eyes were a deep chocolaty brown. His mouth was disturbingly sensual, with a muscular curve on either side to set it off.

By any standards he was exceedingly handsome. Not in a glamour-boy style, but in a rugged masculine way that was matched by his attire. His jeans hugged his body as if loving hands had patted them into place, and his plaid shirt was open at the throat to reveal a twist of dark chest hair.

As she looked at him, the air seemed thick and close, and her knees felt rubbery. Only a tiny part of her recognized that he had been subjecting her to the same intense scrutiny she had unintentionally given him. There had been nothing insulting, merely appreciative, in the way his gaze took in her neat, small features—blue eyes, slightly tip-tilted nose, impudent mouth—and her slim rounded contours.

"I'm sorry," he said apologetically. "I didn't mean to sneak up on you." He glanced around the alcove at the two pool tables lined up side by side like a pair of horses in harness and the racks for the cues attached to one wall. Except for the two of them, the alcove was empty. "It doesn't look as if there're very many pool players in this town," he said lightly.

"Enough," Cassie said tersely and instantly realized how ungracious she must have sounded.

He frowned, drawing his dark brows together. "I'm sorry. I should have realized you didn't want to be disturbed."

No brains. No manners. No common sense, either. If she had any of the latter, she'd embellish on her inadvertent rudeness and make this man go away. But she couldn't bring herself to do it. "I'm awfully sorry, uh..." She broke off, wishing she had paid more attention when Doc Anderson, on his last visit to her place, had mentioned his replacement's name.

The vet picked up on her uncertainty and extended his hand. "It's Dan. Dan Faraday."

Without intending to, Cassie replied formally, like a little girl acting out a parent's careful coaching. "How do you do, Doctor Faraday. I'm Cassie McLean."

She couldn't just ignore his hand. She had to shake it, even though she could guess what might be in store. Her fingers slid into his and it happened, just as she feared it would. A sizzling sensation rippled up her arm, dissipating eventually in a much-too-pleasant warmth. His long fingers remained wrapped around hers a bit longer than strictly necessary, and she knew he felt it, too.

It wouldn't do to enjoy it, she cautioned herself. She deliberately envisioned him with a sign pinned to his chest. Doc A's TEMPORARY Replacement, it read, and the word *temporary* was about four times the size of the rest.

Pulling her hand back, she said, "I'm sorry. What I said about there being enough pool players... Well, it just came out wrong, that's all. Do you ever have that happen to you, Doctor Faraday?"

Fool, she thought. Of course, he didn't. He didn't look the type ever to feel confusion or to let his tongue run ahead of his brain. Along with his intense masculinity was a take-charge aura that proclaimed this man was in control... of himself, of his environment, of his life.

But he said easily, "All the time. Don't think anything of it." A quizzical frown etched a fine line across his brow. "Why do you keep calling me 'Doctor'?"

"You *are* a doctor, aren't you?"

"I'm a veterinarian, yes. But I don't understand how you knew."

Cassie gave a little laugh. "I guess you aren't used to living in a small town, Doc. Everyone knows everything in Pinetop." She glanced toward the main room. "You see, most of the people here tonight are locals. The tourists don't come to this place much. And they don't get that great a welcome when they do happen to wander in. The Pizza Bar's kind of a private place, just for the folks who live here year-round."

"I'm not sure I quite understand, Cassie. Are you trying to tell me that I shouldn't have come here?"

Oh Lord! She'd done it again. Made him feel unwelcome when she was only trying to explain. A part of her said that her big mouth and foolish tongue were actually on the right track. For her own preservation, she ought to find a way of keeping this man as far from her as possible. But it seemed unfair to make him feel the outcast for her own selfish interests. Unfair to him and unfair to the genuinely hospitable people of Pinetop. Tourists were a different breed, but Dan Faraday, as Doc Anderson's replacement, would be treated as home folks by the home folks.

"That's not what I meant," she said apologetically. "Naturally you count as a local since you're helping out Doc Anderson and all. I was just trying to explain why I knew who you are . . . why everybody knows who you are."

His frown smoothed away, and the beginnings of a smile bent the corners of his lips. "I see. Please go on."

Dan Faraday was fascinated by this glimpse of the workings of small-town life. He had known it would be different from L.A., but he had a hunch he was only getting his first tiny taste of how very different the flavor would turn out to be.

But if he had been forced to tell the truth about his thoughts and feelings at that moment, he was even more fascinated by the petite young woman who was lecturing him, as if she were the town's official tour guide.

Earlier, across the room, he had happened to glance toward the alcove. Something had happened. Dan wasn't exactly sure what. A momentary ripple in the atmosphere, perhaps. A dislocation of the usual and the ordinary that had taken place when his gaze fell on Cassie. That same force, whatever it was, had drawn him toward the pool table just as soon as he was able to get free from the people who seemed bent on welcoming him to Pinetop.

Now that he was here, the pull toward her was even stronger. He had rarely experienced it before to this degree, but he recognized it—an instant chemical attraction between him and Cassie McLean.

Or call it a good old-fashioned case of lust, he thought ironically.

At the same time he was getting conflicting vibrations from her. Not only a pull, but a definite push. One second he had the feeling she wished he would vanish in a puff of smoke. The next he thought just the opposite, that she wouldn't mind a bit if he were to move closer.

And all of it was crazy. The mountain air must be getting to him. He wasn't the sort to dwell on the complicated nuances of human behavior. He'd always been a pretty straightforward kind of guy. And life had always gone pretty straightforwardly for him. At least, until recently.

But then, he'd never expected to find himself—however temporarily—taking over a general practice in a hick, one-vet town like Pinetop. With his entire life askew, it was no wonder he was experiencing mental aberrations.

"I don't know exactly how the word got around who you were," Cassie was saying. "Somebody must have seen you unloading your stuff at Doc Anderson's."

Dan nodded. "I spent most of the afternoon going in and out, carrying things in from my van."

"Well, there you are. Somebody probably saw you and figured you must be the new vet. So then, whoever saw you probably said to somebody else, 'The new horse doctor's in town.' And then when you walked in here tonight, somebody recognized you, told somebody else and that's it."

Dan laughed. "So that's how it works. Thanks for the education."

It was getting tougher and tougher for Cassie, having him standing so near, watching her as if every word she said enthralled him. "How about some pool?" she suggested. At least playing would enable her to move around the table and away from him.

"Sure, I'll take you on," he said easily. "I haven't played since college, though. I'll bet I'm pretty rusty."

"Sure, Doc," she scoffed. "That's what all the pool hustlers say."

He took a cue from the rack on the wall, then picked up a cake of rosin. "Is everybody in Pinetop going to call me Doc?"

"Probably. Why? Don't you like it?"

"I don't dislike it, exactly. I'm just not used to it." He put down the rosin. "You don't suppose *you* could call me Dan?"

Cassie actually had to consider for a moment. Calling him by his first name seemed such a little thing. Yet it was a step toward him, not away from him. And it was the latter direction she ought to be heading at a full gallop. But she said, "Sure . . . Dan."

Just then, Jack Webley strode into the alcove, the heels of his cowboy boots tapping on the wooden floor. He planted his hands on his hips and said boisterously, "Hey, Doc! What're you doing fooling around with my best girl?"

A scowl momentarily crossed Dan Faraday's face.

Cassie blurted indignantly, "I'm no such thing, Jack Webley, and you know it." Almost at once, she realized that she *could* have let the devastating new doctor think she was spoken for. Only it would have done no good. He would soon find out the truth.

She turned to Dan. "Don't pay any attention to his foolishness, Doc...uh, Dan. To hear Jack talk, every unattached female in town is his 'best girl.'" She paused. "I'm sorry. I guess I ought to introduce the two of you."

Dan smiled, a wider, brighter smile than seemed strictly warranted by the occasion. "There's no need. Jack and I have already met." He set his cue down on the green felt surface of the table, then leaned back against the rack that held the pool cues. "So tell me, Jack. Is Cassie *anybody's* best girl?"

Jack shook his head. "Nope. But it's not for lack of trying by most of the young fellows around here. And a few of the old codgers, too, to tell the truth."

Cassie protested, "That's a lie, Jack Webley, and you know it."

Dan's gaze flickered appreciatively over her. "If it *is* a lie, then the mountain air must do awful things to people's eyesight."

"Oh, no, Doc," Jack said. "Lotsa fellas got twenty-twenty vision up here. Hasn't done them no good with Cassie, though."

Dan's eyes met Jack's in a conspiratorial glance. No matter how different the two men seemed, it was obvious to Cassie they had become instant allies. She glared at one, then the other, but they pretended to take no notice.

"She spurns them all, does she?"

"Sure does, Doc. She's mighty particular."

"Is that so?"

Jack nodded vigorously. "*Mighty* particular. Ain't nobody from around here been good enough for her yet."

"That's interesting," Dan said heartily. "Please go on."

Men, Cassie thought disgustedly. It wasn't quite locker room conversation—the words were too polite—but it was the next thing to it.

As Jack chuckled and said, "Ain't nothin' to go on about. That's what I've been trying to tell you," Cassie's lips firmed and her small rounded chin jutted. Back rigid, she turned and stalked stiff-legged away from the pool table.

When she was just outside the alcove, Jack called, "Hey, Cassie, where're you going?"

She slowed her stride only a fraction and called back over her shoulder, "To go talk to people who have some notion of civil conversation. If you 'boys' get done shooting the breeze and decide you want to shoot some pool instead, give me a call."

2

DAN FARADAY WATCHED the slim figure blend into the crowd around the bar. "Damn!" he muttered under his breath.

Jack Webley gave him a quizzical look, then pulled his brown felt cowboy hat down so it shaded his eyes. "Don't you worry none, Doc. Cassie's quick to get her dander up, but she calms down just as quick. You'll see."

"I hope you're right," Dan said. He was disgusted with himself—with the way he had encouraged Jack to talk abou. Cassie as if she weren't even there.

Jack shot a keen glance at Dan from under his hat brim. "You're really bothered, aren't you, Doc?"

Dan made a noncommittal sound.

Jack studied the floor, where the toe of his boot was drawing a circular pattern. "Ain't none of my business, really. But if you're thinking you might give Cassie a go, maybe you'd better think again. Like I was trying to tell you before, Cassie doesn't fool around."

"I'm glad to hear it," Dan said pleasantly. Jack's news was no deterrent as far as he was concerned. At thirty-two, he wasn't interested in women who went for short-term flings or—even worse—one-night stands. The risks were too high, the rewards too meager. And if Jack meant, as he seemed to, that Cassie hadn't been involved with anyone for quite some time, then living in Pinetop could account for it. There probably weren't a whole lot of single men around. If none of them was right for her, as he guessed might be the case, then good for her that she hadn't simply made do with what was available.

And you think you're right for her, do you, Dan? inquired a sneering little voice in his head. *That's a bit conceited, isn't it?*

Well, maybe it was, he mentally countered. But, damn it, yes, he did think he might be right for her. Just looking at her and talking to her for a few minutes had given him the hunch that between them was something nice, waiting to be developed.

Jack shrugged as if to say, "Well, I warned you," then went on. "There's another thing, Doc. Couldn't it get kind of complicated, Cassie being your best customer and all?"

Dan frowned. "My best customer? Cassie? What do you mean?"

"She didn't tell you?"

"She didn't have a chance to tell me much of anything."

"Why, Cassie owns the livery stable. Pinetop Stable, it's called. Right on the main road. You must've seen it when you drove into town."

Dan winced. He had seen it all right. A dilapidated old property with sagging fences and graying, unpainted boards. He'd grimaced at it, automatically disapproving of the person who would house horses in such a place. And now that person turned out to be the woman who attracted him more than he'd been attracted to any woman in a long, long time.

He said to Jack, "Cassie owns *that* place?"

"Yep. Been runnin' it on her own for four years now, ever since her daddy died."

"I see," he said slowly. It *was* a complication, though not necessarily the kind Jack seemed to think. There was no rule forbidding a veterinarian a personal relationship with his patients' owners. But if Cassie's animals weren't properly cared for, he'd never be able to keep quiet about it. Which wasn't likely to endear him to her.

And as far as endearing went, he was already batting zero, he thought. Under the circumstances it was probably just as well. But then . . . He glanced toward the crowd in the main room and caught a glimpse of her golden-brown hair, her pert profile. There was that pull again, urging him in her direction. He'd never felt anything quite like it before, and he decided he owed it to himself to find out what it meant.

Thrusting aside the thought of the ramshackle old stable she owned, he said to Jack, "If you'll excuse me, I think I'll go apologize to Cassie for the way we were talking."

"Suit yourself, Doc." Jack shrugged and picked up a pool cue as Dan walked away.

CASSIE SAT ON A BAR STOOL, the toes of her sneakers poised on the railing that ran around the bottom of the bar. Beside her was her best friend, Mary Jo Cooper.

Predictably Mary Jo had wanted to discuss the new Doc, how attractive he was, what people had said about him. But each time Cassie had firmly cut her off.

Now she shot a keen glance at the ponytailed blonde. "Honest to goodness, Mary Jo, I don't know why you won't put Jack Webley out of his misery."

Mary Jo put on her hurt Southern belle face—all injured innocence. "Why, whatever are you talking about, Cassie McLean?" She even managed a hint of a drawl. Quite a feat, since she'd never been any farther from Pinetop than Los Angeles, a mere hundred and fifty miles away. Pinetop might be located in Southern California, but that hardly accounted for Mary Jo's air of magnolias and mint juleps.

Cassie closed her fingers around the half-full beer glass on the counter in front of her. "Don't try to kid me, Mary Jo. We've known each other since we were in diapers. *I* know you're crazy about Jack. *You* know you're crazy about Jack. The whole town knows you're crazy about Jack."

The whole town also knew that Mary Jo had spent more than a few nights at Jack's cabin outside of town. Yet the blonde still behaved capriciously—flirting with other men in public on occasion, sometimes acting as if she and Jack were mere acquaintances.

"The only one who doesn't know for sure is Jack," Cassie said. "I don't see why you keep tormenting him the way you do."

Mary Jo bit on her lower lip. "I do care about him, Cassie. A lot."

"Thank heaven," Cassie said with an exaggerated sigh. "Do you realize this is the first time you've admitted it . . . even to me?"

"If you ever tell Jack what I said, I'll say you're lying," Mary Jo said fiercely.

"Okay, okay." Cassie held up her hands in a helpless gesture. "But *why*? I'd think you'd want him to know how you feel."

"Sometimes I do," Mary Jo admitted. "Sometimes I even start thinking about marriage and babies. You know, the wedding and the cottage with the white picket fence, and it all sounds real pretty."

"So? If I know Jack—and I do know Jack, remember?— then it sounds pretty good to him, too. What's the problem?"

Mary Jo took a dainty sip of her gin and tonic. "So then I start thinking about the rest of it. Dirty diapers and being chained to the house all day long, tied down for years and years. And Jack getting bald—his hair's getting thin on top already—and fat and maybe not making me laugh anymore and then I . . ." Her voice trailed away.

Cassie murmured into her beer, "I know what you mean."

Mary Jo's delicately arched eyebrows rose. "You do? Are you sweet on somebody, Cassie? I had no idea."

"Of course I'm not," she said defensively. She couldn't be sweet on a man she'd only just met, a man she didn't know at all. Could she? "I just meant that I know what you mean about the babies and being tied down and all."

She had seen it happen to other young women in Pinetop. After a few years of marriage, some of them looked tired and worn, pinched and harried. Others still retained the radiance of their wedding day, augmented by a glow of contentment. The difference, Cassie had concluded, was caused by numerous factors. But the most important was whether or not wife and husband were in love. That was one reason Cassie herself had never been tempted to take up with any of Pinetop's few eligible males. Without that spark, that glow of love, marriage could turn into drudgery and defeat. With it, though . . . ah, that was something else again.

At twenty-eight she knew she ought to be worrying good and hard about finding a mate and settling down. She did worry, sometimes, when the clock struck midnight on a Saturday night and she was home alone. But desperation was no substitute for love and she knew it.

"But if you really love Jack," she said earnestly, "then it wouldn't be that way. And Jack's a good man. I'm sure it'd work out just fine."

"Maybe. Maybe not," Mary Jo said thoughtfully. "Anyway, there's more to it than that. You know me, Cassie. You know how I get to thinking about the whole big world out there, away from Pinetop. Cities. Glamorous people doing exciting things. Sometimes I think I ought to leave Pinetop and not come back for a long time."

Cassie shook her head. "You wouldn't like it, Mary Jo. Take my word for it."

"You always say the same thing, Cass. Just because you hated it when you went to school in L.A., doesn't mean that I'd hate it, too."

"Yes, you would," Cassie said darkly. She had learned things in L.A.; she couldn't deny that. She'd gained a wider experience of the world, which was why her father had wanted her to go to art school in the city. But she had also learned that city relationships were rarely for keeps. In cities, people rushed around all the time, seeking out the new. New restaurants, new fads, new loves.

She turned to Mary Jo. "You know what they say. It's a great place to visit—only I don't even agree with that. You can't breathe and you can't find your way around on the freeways and there's no place to walk where your feet aren't hitting concrete." She wrinkled her nose. "A city's a good place to go shopping when you can't find what you need right here in Pinetop . . . and that's about all it's good for, as far as I'm concerned."

"You never think about going back?" Mary Jo asked.

"They'd have to carry me there on a stretcher."

"Or maybe going someplace else, not so big as L.A., but bigger than Pinetop?"

"Why should I? I've got everything I want right here." With one noticeable exception, Cassie thought. A man to call her own, to love and care about. But that was a dilemma she'd have to live with. And then she realized how unusual it was for her to brood over her single state as much as she was doing tonight. Usually she was quite content. Her life was full, her days busy. Many of her evenings were spent with friends. If she was occasionally lonely, it was a loneliness she had managed to fill with activities.

She knew why she was thinking those thoughts, though. The party responsible was over in the alcove with Jack Webley.

But a quick glance in that direction proved he wasn't. And then she saw him, his dark head visible above most of the crowd as he moved toward the bar.

He reached them a moment later. Mary Jo swiveled on her stool and said brightly, "Well, hello again, Doc!"

Cassie nodded a greeting, smiling slightly. By now she had forgotten to be mad. She had also forgotten the full, undiluted force of Dan Faraday's appeal. With him standing so near, his shoulders seemed even broader, his hips leaner, legs longer. She noticed there was a slight indentation in his chin—not quite a dimple, exactly, but something it might be all too pleasant to trace with her fingertip. The masculine roughness of his skin, the faint scent of his after-shave and an even fainter perfume she might dub Eau de Male all added up to a potent intoxicant.

"Hello...Mary Jo, isn't it?" he said pleasantly, but his gaze quickly returned to Cassie's face.

Mary Jo's eyes darted from Cassie to Dan. "Well, if you'll excuse me . . ." She let out a little giggle. "Why do I get the feeling my presence won't be missed?"

Cassie hardly heard her, hardly noticed Mary Jo slip off the bar stool and edge away through the crowd.

"I'm sorry," Dan said. "I didn't mean to chase her away."

Cassie grinned. "Yes, you did."

His smile broke out again, doing devastating things to Cassie's composure. "Okay. I did. I hope she doesn't mind."

Mary Jo, Cassie was pleased to note, was heading toward the alcove . . . and Jack. "I'm sure she doesn't."

Dan glanced at the unoccupied bar stool. "Okay if I join you?"

"Be my guest."

He stepped up onto the stool, then rested his elbows on the bar, which put his hands and muscular forearms right in Cassie's line of sight. There was a feathering of dark hairs on his arms, on the backs of his hands and lightly decorating the tops of his long fingers. His hands were well made, with blunt fingertips, and his nails, she noticed, were very clean. She wasn't used to seeing a man with such clean hands. Pinetop's males tended to carry around a residue of their—mostly outdoor—occupations. For some reason, that cleanliness didn't make Dan Faraday seem citified, or sissy...just appealing.

An earnest brusqueness clipped his words. "Look, Cassie. I want to apologize."

"What for?" she said, genuinely astonished.

"The way I was talking about you with Jack. It was unforgivable."

The corners of her lips twitched with amusement. "Yes, it was, wasn't it?" Now she knew she was dealing with a different breed. No Pinetop male would ever have apologized for a little bantering over a woman. "But it's okay. You're forgiven."

His grin was wide, crinkling the corners of his eyes and revealing straight white teeth. "Whew!" he said, swiping one hand across his brow. "That's a relief! Can I buy you a beer as a peace offering?"

She glanced at her glass, which was still a quarter full. "No thanks. As a matter of fact, I think I'd better get going." Her common sense reminded her it wouldn't be smart to sit around chit-chatting with this too appealing male for any longer than necessary. Besides, it was late and she had to get up early. The horses expected a nice flake of hay first thing, while the sun was still a golden glow around the dark silhouette of Rainbow Peak. And flakes of hay rarely got themselves up and deposited themselves in corrals and stalls.

Dan glanced at his watch. "You're right. It is getting late, isn't it? I guess I'd better take off, too. Why don't I walk you to your car?"

Cassie slid off the bar stool. "Thanks, but I don't have a car . . . not here, I mean. I walked up from my place."

"Your place?"

"Jack didn't tell you? I own the Pinetop Stable." She chuckled. "I don't *live* in the stable, of course. The house is in back."

"But that must be a mile from here!"

"Not even close." Seeing his expression of disbelief, she admitted, "Three-quarters of a mile, maybe."

"You can't intend to walk all that way in the dark. It isn't safe."

A wry grin curved Cassie's lips. "It's easy to tell you're a city fellow. It's safe as can be. Especially in the winter when there aren't so many damn fool tourists around."

"Well, maybe," he said uncertainly. "But won't you freeze to death?"

"My jacket's hanging over by the door. Got a scarf in the pocket and most likely a pair of gloves. I'll be fine."

"Humor me," he urged. "Let me drive you home. I walked over here myself, but my van's just down the street at Doc Anderson's house."

Cassie wavered. It *had* been cold when she arrived at the Pizza Bar. By now it would be colder, dark, perhaps a wind blowing. "I wouldn't want to put you to any trouble."

"It's no trouble. You wait here. I'll go get the van. Be back in a minute."

She looked up at him, surprise widening her eyes. "The women you're used to must be pretty delicate blossoms. I'll take you up on that offer of a ride, but I sure can walk to Doc's with you. Half a block!"

Dan pondered her words for a moment. He had never considered Audrey delicate. The woman he had been seeing before the debacle that had turned his life upside down and eventually landed him here in Pinetop was a tall, command-

ing brunette. She was hardly the clinging vine type, which
was one of the things he had liked about her. Practically the
only thing, he had discovered as soon as she said goodbye.

He recalled being out with Audrey and walking blocks
alone to drive the car back to a restaurant to pick her up. She
might not have been a delicate blossom, but she *was* spoiled,
he realized. And Cassie McLean was anything but. He liked
that. Liked it a lot. At the same time, it might be fun to spoil
her a little, to show her that it wasn't necessary for a woman
to be strong and independent *all* the time.

He was jumping the gun, though, assuming that he'd
eventually have the chance and the right to do nice things for
Cassie. But he was still getting the same push-pull feeling
from her facial expressions and body language—as if she felt
some of the same attraction that he did, but really didn't *want*
to. Attraction and resistance. Back and forth. Maybe she was
a little shy, he thought, then realized that didn't fit with anything else he'd seen about her.

He said, "Okay. If you're ready, let's go."

WITH AN OVERSIZED lumberman's jacket to snuggle in and a
woolly scarf wrapped around her ears, Cassie scarcely felt
the cold as she strolled down Pinetop's main street beside
Dan. Strolled comfortably, she realized. He had automatically modulated his much longer stride so she wasn't forced
to scurry to keep up. The instinctive courtesy was rare in a
man. Just one more thing to appreciate about Dan Faraday,
she thought.

Don't go appreciating too much, Cassie McLean! There
could be a million pluses in one column, and it took only a
single minus to cancel them all out. He was supposed to be
temporary. A temporary replacement for Doc Anderson was
what she had heard. But Pinetop gossip was not infre-
quently wrong. Maybe it wasn't true. How much she hoped

it wasn't true was disconcerting, considering that she scarcely knew the man.

She glanced at Dan and caught him in a swiftly controlled shiver. His fashionable, beige windbreaker wouldn't be doing much to keep out the chill night air.

"You'll need more than that when the snows come," she observed.

Dan shoved his hands more deeply in his pockets. "I guess I will. I hadn't really thought about it. It's been a while since I've had to cope with cold winters."

"Where are you from, Dan? I don't remember Doc Anderson saying."

"L.A. For the past five years, anyway."

Consternation was evident in Cassie's voice. "L.A."

They had reached the corner. Dan instinctively stopped to look across the street, then realized that Cassie hadn't even slowed her pace. No traffic problem—that he could get used to easily, he thought. He caught up with her and asked, "Something wrong with my being from L.A.?"

She said casually, "Work with mostly dogs and cats, did you?"

Dan's chuckle reverberated on the silent street. "I get it. You're afraid I'm not competent with horses."

They came to a stop in front of Doc Anderson's place. It was a low, wide building faced with knotty pine. The office was at one end, living quarters at the other. The house part was small, a little cramped, but perfectly adequate, Dan had decided, for the few months he expected to be in Pinetop.

He turned to face her, and to hide her embarrassment, she looked over his shoulder, pretending to study the black silhouette of the pine tree in Doc Anderson's front yard. "Well, wouldn't you worry if you were me?"

"I suppose I would." His dark eyes twinkled with amusement. "However, it's not the horses, it's Pinetop's dogs and

cats you should be worrying about." Seeing her look of incomprehension, he said gently, "For the past five years, Cassie, one hundred percent of my practice has been with the
genus Equus. I've been boning up on small animal care,
though, rereading my old college texts and all the latest articles."

Cassie stared at him. "Your practice was on horses? In
L.A.? I don't understand."

"I worked as a racehorse vet for various owners and trainers who quartered their horses at the Santa Theresita Race
Track. I had one major client, though . . ." His voice trailed
away.

Once or twice, in the weeks since the incident, Dan had almost wished he'd handled the situation differently that day
when he'd opposed Owen Winwood. But one day or another would have made no difference in the long run. Sooner
or later he would have butted heads with Winwood, the
nephew who had taken charge of Willow Run Racing Stables after Arthur Winwood died. The old man had been Dan's
friend and mentor. But unlike his uncle, Owen hadn't given
a damn what happened to the horses . . . as long as they won.

Even if Dan had guessed what was going to happen—that
Owen Winwood's nasty tales would be believed by the other
owners and trainers for whom he worked, that he would find
himself shut out, unemployed, silently blacklisted—he still
couldn't have acted differently.

It was almost incidental that along with everything else,
he'd also lost Audrey. Once she discovered he was no longer
part of the glamorous racing world, she had walked out of
his life. What Dan found most interesting about that particular aspect of the whole messy, tragic situation was how little he had cared.

Cassie watched the twinkle fade from Dan's eyes to be replaced by something lost looking, with perhaps a hint of an-

ger. He was silent for a long moment, then pointed toward the sky. It was ablaze with stars, the high altitude and clear, thin air bringing the heavens near, as if the keeper of the celestial dome had lowered it a bit so paltry humans could get a closer look. "Look at that. I've never seen so many stars."

As usual, the sky was gorgeous, Cassie thought. But Dan's sudden interest was obviously motivated by a desire to change the subject. Something about racehorses, something about his previous work was eating at him. She shouldn't push it, she decided. It was none of her business, anyway.

Dan pulled his car keys from his pocket. "Shall we be on our way?"

She waited until the van was on the main road to ask, "So what do you think of Pinetop so far?"

"It seems nice. With only half a day's experience of the place, it's hard to tell."

"You didn't visit before you agreed to take over from Doc Anderson?"

He gave her a teasing glance, then returned his attention to the road. "You don't know? I thought everyone knew everything around here."

"Sometimes communications break down a mite," she admitted.

"It's nice to know the Pinetop telegraph isn't infallible. No, I didn't visit. I was looking for something temporary. When I saw Doctor Anderson's ad, it seemed like the perfect thing to do for a while."

There it was. What she had wanted to know . . . and didn't want to know. At least it answered her most pressing question. No matter how appealing this man was, she wasn't going to get involved. Not even an inch involved. Not even a touch or a solitary kiss. She had too much self-esteem to subject herself to the inevitable disappointment.

"You're not thinking about buying Doc Anderson's practice, then," she said slowly. She knew the older man was anxious to sell.

"Good heavens, no! It's just until . . ."

"Until what?"

"Until it seems like the right time to go back to racing," Dan said flatly. Again, there was a warning in his voice. Stay away; this hurts, it said. Then his face smoothed. "Or until Doctor Anderson sells his practice. Whichever comes first."

"I see." Now it was Cassie's voice that had gone flat. Why was she belaboring the point, anyway? He had said he was temporary, and that was that.

Something he had said bothered her, Dan realized. He couldn't think what it was, but he had sensed a definite withdrawal.

She remained quiet and, in Dan's opinion, the distance to her place went all too quickly. He made the turn into the dirt parking lot in front of the Pinetop Stable.

A full moon rode high in the sky, illuminating Cassie's domain. Behind the parking area was a large, empty riding ring and behind that, the stable building itself. It was constructed like a barn, with a high pitched roof. The double doors would open, Dan could guess, onto a central aisle with stalls on either side. Off to one side of the structure was a large corral where perhaps a dozen horses dozed. And deep in the property, nestled into the woods, was a small clapboard house.

Dan glanced over at Cassie, forgetting all about his disapproval of the stable. The same moon that turned the graying wood of wall and fences to luminescent silver seemed to caress her cheeks and lend her eyes an added glow. Her golden-brown hair looked touchably soft. He would have liked to smooth the feathery wisps with his fingertips. Right now, for instance.

He reached out. But at the last moment he got a grip on himself, and his hand detoured to her shoulder. His touch was light, a tentative question. "Cassie?" he said gently and began to lean toward her.

She leaned away from him, her body language making a definite statement. "Didn't Jack tell you, Doc? I don't fool around."

Dan took his hand from her shoulder. "He did tell me, as a matter of fact. Funny coincidence. I don't fool around, either."

"Why do I get the feeling you and I don't mean the same thing when we say that?"

"Beats me. A minor problem in semantics, maybe. I'm sure we'll be able to work it out." Without meaning to, he found himself leaning toward her again, as if he were a needle to her north.

But north was on the move. Cassie's hand dropped to the door handle and pushed. She shoved the door open and hopped out of the van. From the ground, she looked up at him. "About that 'working out,'" she said. "I'm going to do you a favor and tell you right up front . . . it's not going to happen, Doc."

Before Dan could respond, she turned and strode away. He watched her silhouette cross the yard, waited until he heard a door open and close again. He wasn't the kind of man to force his attentions on a woman who had as good as said she wasn't interested. But there was so much else about her that said otherwise. The light in her eyes when she looked at him. The way she smiled. And besides, he thought, the current of attraction he felt flowing between them was too strong to be completely one-sided.

He shifted the van into reverse, muttering aloud, "We'll just see about that, Miss Cassie McLean. We'll just see about that."

3

CASSIE OPENED the kitchen door of her house and stepped outside onto the back porch. It was a chilly morning, heralding the true winter cold. The puff of breath she blew out made a small cloud in the air, and there was frost on the brown grass in the garden.

I wonder if Dan's gotten himself some mountain clothes, yet. It was an idle thought, an intrusive thought, and she pushed it firmly aside. She had been doing her best not to think about Dan Faraday, and she had managed pretty well . . . most of the time. Luck had been with her; she hadn't seen him at all in the week since he drove her home. Luck and some deliberate effort. She had kept away from town, except for a quick visit to the bakery and the grocery store, and the horses had cooperated by staying in perfect health.

Cassie looked back through the open doorway. "Come on, Blunder," she called to the black-and-white border collie curled up under the kitchen table. "Time for us to get to work."

The dog got to his feet and stretched, white forepaws extended, black rump high in the air. Waving his white-plumed tail, he trotted outside to join his mistress.

Off to the side of the house, pine forest climbed a gentle slope that continued on and on for miles, growing steeper as it neared the timberline. A small garden, mostly barren now, lay between the porch and the back of the stable. At the end of an unpaved drive that led around from the parking lot, Cassie's pickup truck was parked next to a shed where she stored hay and grain and the straw that cushioned the floors of the stalls.

With Blunder trotting after her, she walked briskly to the door of the shed. Inside, hay in rectangular bales was stacked high against the walls.

Falling easily into her twice-daily routine, she clipped the wire on a new bale of hay and separated it into individual sections, or flakes, each one a couple of inches thick. Then she stacked a dozen flakes on a flat-bottomed, four-wheeled cart. The cart had once been painted green, but now it was green and rust-colored in about equal measure.

As Cassie worked, Blunder sniffed inquisitively in the dark corners. He showed no particular excitement, which was good. Keeping rats and mice out of the feed was a constant battle, but not a battle she would have to fight today, thank heaven.

With the cart piled high and the hay fork balanced on top, she maneuvered the unwieldy vehicle out of the shed. After sliding open the double doors at the back of the barn, she wheeled the cart down the wide central aisle. Low whickers of interest and the sounds of stamping feet came from the stalls. Equine heads appeared in the open top halves of the doors on either side, eyes expressing resentment, Cassie fancied.

"You know the rules, guys," she said. "Your buddies in the corral get fed before you do." She liked getting the longest trek with the cart out of the way first. And besides, she thought it only fair that the animals who had to stay out in the elements should breakfast before the more privileged creatures inside.

As they came to the end of the stable nearest the tack room, Blunder swerved in front of her to sniff at the door of an empty stall. Making a mental note to check the stall for rodents, Cassie called the dog to her side, then pushed the cart out the front doors.

Hearing the approach of the chow wagon, ten horses and two small shaggy ponies shoved together in a clump near the gate of the corral. Nearer the road was the arena where boarders—and Cassie herself—could work their horses and where, in tourist time, she sometimes offered pony rides.

Cassie trundled the cart around the side of the corral on a dirt pathway worn smooth by thousands of such morning and evening trips. The horses inside followed her to the section of fence where she would unload the flakes of hay.

Now was the tricky part. She had to move quickly to deposit all the flakes in a line along the fence or some animals might be cheated, while the greedy ones got more than their fair share.

She picked up the hay fork. Her hands and wrists were strong from years of riding and working with horses. She flipped the flakes of hay between two fence rails, one after another until the cart was bare.

"Not bad this morning," she murmured. As usual, the horses jostled and shoved for position. Banjo, the tall bay mare, challenged one of the ponies for a particularly desirable flake . . . and won. Sometimes fights broke out, hooves flying in warning kicks as one animal reestablished dominance over another. But this morning the process was relatively serene.

Cassie propped her bent arms on the topmost fence rail. "I'm sure going to miss you guys when you're gone," she observed to the uninterested horses.

It was time to send the horses in the corral down the mountain to the flat desert lands below. The next morning, Fred Hanson would drive his six-horse trailer into the yard to take the first load of animals to the winter pasture Cassie rented from an obliging rancher. After Fred's second trip in the afternoon, only the stabled horses would remain—five that belonged to Cassie, including Kettle, her pride and joy, and the four she boarded. The ones of hers left in the barn would suffice for the few winter rental customers.

With the number of animals reduced, her life would become relatively leisurely. She loved winter for the time it gave her. Time to work with Kettle, when the weather was clear. Time to paint. Time to accomplish little projects around the house and stable. So she would be both glad and sorry to say goodbye to her friends who lived in the corral.

Mostly sorry, though. Every year, she felt as if she were losing part of her family. But the horses who went to pasture would enjoy a warmer climate and a place to run free until, in the spring, the trailer brought them back up the mountain to resume their duties.

The corral horses were contentedly munching their hay. Cassie reminded herself to make a later check of the automatic devices that bubbled up water at the push of an equine nose, then turned the cart and pushed it back into the stable.

At once, Blunder detoured to the empty stall that had interested him earlier. Pushing his nose against a crack between two boards, he made a high-pitched whine of doggy discontent.

Cassie frowned. "What is it, pup?" Leaving the cart in the middle of the aisle, she went to the stall and peered into the dim interior. In a back corner was what looked like an abandoned bundle of rags.

She opened the door of the stall and stepped inside. The smell of stale whiskey and cigarettes assailed her nostrils, and the bundle in the corner let out a moan. She hesitated only a moment before stepping forward to bend over the sleeping man.

"Willie!" she exclaimed. Willie Wilson, a wiry little gray-haired man, worked for her part-time during the busy season. In the winter, he, like the corral horses, headed for a warmer climate—Banning or Beaumont or one of the other desert towns.

She touched his shoulder. Up close, the smell of whiskey made her stomach turn, and she frowned as she saw the half dozen cigarette butts stubbed out on the stall floor.

She knew Willie sometimes drank. Occasionally she had smelled it on his breath, and there were days when he didn't show up for work. But she had never seen him like this. Nor had she realized that he smoked. Probably he didn't, except when he was drinking heavily, she thought. The smoking worried her more than the alcohol. Smoking around a stable, with highly flammable hay just waiting to be set alight, was a serious violation of her safety rules.

Willie's eyelids fluttered. "Willie, wake up." She gently shook his shoulder. "Are you all right?"

He stirred and moaned again. There was white stubble on his cheeks and chin, and his clothing reeked of spilt whiskey. At the best of times, Willie was a little grimy around the edges, but now he looked like an old derelict, sleeping it off on a street corner in L.A. Her feelings ricocheted between pity and alarm at the danger he might have caused her horses.

"Wake up, Willie," she repeated.

He mumbled, "What—Who—" then rolled over so he was lying on his back, his eyes blinking as he tried to focus.

"It's me. Cassie."

Slowly he maneuvered himself into a sitting position. Her anxiety receding now that he had shown himself capable of movement, Cassie let her tone resonate with severity. "What are you doing here, Willie?"

He shook his head gingerly, as if he feared it might topple to the floor. "Aw, dang it, Cassie," he said ruefully. "I meant to be out of here by the time you started feeding. It was too cold last night for sleeping rough."

"Sleeping rough? I thought you stayed in the Hendersons' cabin."

"They won't let me sleep there no more."

She didn't say so, but she guessed that the Hendersons—summer people—must have visited their cabin unexpectedly and found Willie drunk. She said briskly, "Well, you can't sleep here, either. It's too cold." She hated to be cruel to the old man, but it *was* too cold and getting colder every day. "And you know you shouldn't smoke in a barn. You know how dangerous it is."

Willie winced, and Cassie couldn't find in her heart to go on chastising him. "Never mind," she said kindly. "There was no harm done . . . this time. Why don't you go in the house? There's some coffee on the stove. You'll feel better when you've had some . . . and maybe washed up a little."

He nodded eagerly. "Okay, Cassie. Whatever you say." He shakily got to his feet, then stumbled past her, out of the stall.

Cassie bent and retrieved the crushed cigarette butts. She should have spoken to him more forcefully, she thought. She really couldn't allow him to bunk in her stable. Not if he was going to smoke or wander around drunk, creating who knew what havoc. She'd have to talk to him about it later and make him understand that she couldn't permit anything like this ever to happen again.

It took her half an hour to feed the horses in the stable and to check that all the automatic waterers were in working order. Next, she would remove the blankets the horses wore at night and start exercising some of the animals. But first, she decided, she was entitled to a short break.

With a handful of sugar lumps in her pocket she walked to the middle stall on the right-hand side. When she was still a dozen feet away, a head poked out of the opening. The chestnut gelding's wide-set, intelligent eyes and narrow muzzle revealed that although his powerful build came from his quarter horse ancestors, the blood of aristocratic Arabians also ran in his veins.

"You knew I was coming to see you, didn't you, Kettle?" Cassie held out her gloved palm for the horse to lip up a sugar cube.

Visiting with Kettle was always a pleasant interlude for Cassie, but today she felt unsettled, as if something was askew in her normally contented existence. She tried to explain it away as worry over Willie, but that was unconvincing. She'd been feeling the same way for days, as if her interior balance had shifted and her usually secure foundations were tilting.

Of course, it might be a touch of loneliness, she thought. She was a fairly sociable creature and drew sustenance from contact with her friends, whose usual meeting place was the Pinetop Pizza Bar. But she hadn't dared to return since the night Dan Faraday walked in.

It was a simple equation. A sensible person avoided dangerous situations and Dan Faraday equaled danger. That night, in his van, it had taken all her strength to keep from letting him kiss her. Her only bulwark, when he leaned toward her with that light in his eyes, had been to remind herself that his presence in Pinetop was only temporary.

She had stayed in L.A. long enough—four years in art school, plus one year afterward working for a small advertising agency—to learn the perils to heart and mind of the short-term affair. Twice, she had experienced one herself. Once with Carl, a talented artist a year ahead of her in school. After graduating, Carl had taken off to New York to pursue fame and fortune, and that was that.

And then, while working at the agency, she had gotten involved with Mac, a young attorney who lived in the same apartment building as she. She had just begun to perceive that

Mac wasn't the kind to become a fixture in any woman's life when the call came to tell her that her father had had a stroke.

Not a bad one, she was assured. His right side was weakened, his speech slightly slurred, but with time and therapy, he should return to relative normality. Of course, in the meantime, there was a problem. It would be a while before he would be fit enough to care for the horses and run the business. Cassie's mother had died when she was three, and she was an only child, so it was up to her.

She had quit her job, told her landlord she was leaving, thrown her possessions in the back of her VW and headed up the mountain. She was worried about her father, but not for a moment on that trip had she felt that his illness was forcing her to do something she didn't want to do. Without knowing it, she realized, she had been looking for an excuse to go home to Pinetop.

She had fitted back into mountain life as if she'd never been away. Her father had made an excellent recovery, and she would always be grateful for the two good years she had with him before his second stroke, the one that killed him.

And for a long time, she had been too busy to notice that Mac had never even called to ask how she was getting along.

Easy come, easy go. That seemed to be the philosophy of love these days. But not for Cassie. Never again. She knew better than to expect any relationship to have up-front guarantees. But she had also vowed never again to let her heart be given where there was not even a remote possibility of permanence.

The lessons she had learned in L.A. were not all negative ones, though. She had also discovered that she was a passionate woman, able to rejoice in her ability to give and receive. But there was no one in Pinetop to ignite her fires, and she was determined to stamp on any spark lit by a man who would only sweep through her life and out again.

Still deep in thought, Cassie gave Kettle a last pat on the nose, then went to the cart and pushed it toward the end of the stable nearest the shed. She was nearly outside when something registered on her preoccupied mind.

Something was wrong, or at least unusual. What was it?

She turned back to gaze the length of the stable. There were heads protruding out of almost every stall, eyes hopeful that she might decide to furnish an extra breakfast this morning. And then she realized. Star's head was noticeably absent. The gray mare, one of Cassie's most reliable trail horses, was usually an avid watcher of stable activities.

Concerned, she walked to Star's stall and looked inside. The chunky little mare stood near the back wall, her head hung low. Her hay, in the feeder near the stall door, was untouched.

"Star. Hey, girl," Cassie called.

The horse paid no attention.

Cassie mentally chastised herself. She should have noticed when she delivered Star's hay that the mare wasn't acting right. And she would have, she thought, if she hadn't been mooning over Dan Faraday.

She went inside the stall and quickly checked the mare. Star's nose was runny, but horses got colds all the time without going off their feed. Cassie could find nothing else wrong, yet she knew, just by looking, that this was a sick horse.

She closed and latched the stall's half door and hurried up the aisle to the tack room at the far end. Western saddles sat on racks. Bridles, halters and coiled ropes hung on pegs on one wall. Open shelves held folded horse blankets, towels, rags, and grooming tools.

Posted next to the phone on the wall was a list that included Doc Anderson's number. Cassie dialed. The voice that answered belonged to Ellen Rogers, a married woman in her late thirties who had worked as Doc Anderson's receptionist and stayed on when Dan Faraday took over the practice.

"Ellen, it's Cassie," she said briskly. "Looks like I've got a sick horse. Can you send the Doc over right away?"

"He's with a patient right now, Cassie. And there're a couple more in the waiting room. Is it an emergency?"

"I . . . I don't know." Star wasn't bleeding to death, or having trouble breathing or pawing at her sides in the agony of colic. "I guess it isn't. But I am worried."

"I'll tell Doc. I imagine he'll be able to make it over to your place in a half hour or so."

As soon as she was off the phone, Cassie took an extra-thick horse blanket from the tack room and substituted it for the regular blanket Star had been wearing. Keeping her warm might not help, but it couldn't hurt, she thought. After that, there was nothing more she could do.

DAN FARADAY PARKED his white van next to the stable. In daylight the place looked even more rundown than it had at night. He frowned. It was a disgrace that horses—any horses, even the nags in the corral—should be kept in a place like this. There would be loose boards, maybe even nails to injure the animals. Now that he thought about it, he was surprised that he had spent a full week in Pinetop without receiving an emergency call.

And yet, he couldn't quite make his annoyance with the place carry over to its owner. During the past week, Cassie McLean had frequently invaded his thoughts. Even when he was stitching up a collie that had had too close an encounter with an indignant rooster or administering a rabies shot to a cheerful mutt, a vision of her face or of her slim figure had intruded.

And over and over again, he had heard echoes of her voice, saying, "It's not going to happen, Doc."

Damn it, why not? He was not vain enough to expect any woman he encountered to fall for him. That would be ridiculous. But this was different. He *knew* Cassie was attracted to him. That new sense of perception he'd had since the first moment he saw her assured him it was so. She was free. He was free. So, why?

He got out of the van and instantly his distaste for his surroundings thrust all other thoughts aside. He was standing at the back of his van, opening the door to retrieve his medical bag, when Cassie came out of the stable. A long-haired black-and-white dog trotted along beside her.

"You're here!" she exclaimed. "I'm so glad. I'm so worried about Star." Then her eyes fastened on his face. "What's the matter, Dan? You look as if you're smelling something bad." Her laugh was strained. "Surely you're used to horse smells."

Thinking of potential danger to the horses, he blurted, "This place could sure use some fixing up." But even as he voiced the criticism, he was feasting on the sight of Cassie. It seemed like forever, instead of a week, since the night they'd met—the last time he'd seen her.

Her face was devoid of makeup. A small piece of hay was caught in the locks that feathered around her face, and most of her body was obscured by a bulky, quilted maroon jacket. Yet he'd never seen a woman whose looks appealed to him more. Her cheeks were pink from the cold air or from exertion—or from both, he guessed. Her legs were slim in the faded jeans she wore. His memory supplied the rest—the softly rounded contour of her breasts, the narrow waist, the firmly rounded derriere . . .

"Is *that* why your nose is all pinched?" she asked. Without waiting for an answer, she said lightly, "I know it isn't exactly gorgeous. I just can't seem to get money ahead for repairs."

"But, Cassie…" He stopped himself. This was not the time for a safety lecture. Nor did he especially feel like delivering one at that moment. What he *felt* like doing would be highly inappropriate behavior. He could imagine her shock if the vet, paying a house call on an ailing horse, were to drop his medical bag to the ground and sweep her into his arms.

In a tight voice, she said, "I know what you're thinking, Dan."

He winced. Was the desire he felt to hold her, touch her, that evident? If he'd realized how much his face was going to give away, he'd have practiced bland expressions in his shaving mirror.

But then she went on, and he realized she was talking about something else entirely. "It's not true. The place is safe. There's nothing that can hurt the horses." As an obvious afterthought, she said, "Or any of the people who come around, either."

He tried not to let his disbelief show. "Let's take a look at this sick horse of yours."

He slammed the back door of the van and fell into step beside Cassie as she turned toward the stable.

Cassie's mind was in a whirl. She wasn't really worried about Dan's reaction to her place. She might not have money for cosmetic frills—like a paint job and new fencing—but she was ever vigilant when it came to the safety of her animals. Twice a week she patrolled, searching every inch of stable, corral and arena for any possible danger. Loosened boards were instantly nailed up again. Nails that showed the slightest sign of working themselves out of the wood were summarily removed and replaced. And once Dan Faraday got a closer look, he would see she was telling the truth.

But the trouble was, she had gotten a closer look at Dan Faraday. Even though she had on principle avoided him, one part of her had thought—hoped—that her first swift reaction to him might have been a temporary aberration, a one-time glitch of the emotions that she would never experience again.

No such luck, Cassie, my girl.

The instant she had seen him, standing at the back of his van, even with his lips thinned to a narrow line and his jaw jutting with disapproval, all kinds of funny things had happened to her insides. And now, simply from his proximity, her heart was beating extra hard.

The pure cold sunlight picked up reddish highlights in his dark brown hair and revealed more clearly than had the dim light at the Pizza Bar his forceful features and the outdoorsy tan of his skin. Not to mention the breadth of his shoulders under a new blue down jacket and the lean strength of his corduroy-trousered thighs. But she had no business thinking of thighs—especially not with Star sick.

Cassie stopped outside the door of the mare's stall. "She hasn't eaten. And you can see how she looks."

Dan went inside the stall. "There, there, old girl," he crooned to the mare. "Not feeling your best, are you?" He slipped off his gloves, thrust them in the pocket of his jacket and stroked the horse's neck. Then he removed the heavy blanket Cassie had put on the mare and hung it over the stall door.

With Blunder sitting attentively nearby, Cassie watched as Dan, uttering wordless soothing sounds, pressed a stethoscope to the horse's ribs. He listened for a moment, then said, "She's sick, all right. But it's nothing to worry about."

The air rushed out of Cassie's lungs. "Thank heaven. Do you know what it is?"

"If you want it in doctorese, it's an equine upper respiratory viral infection."

"You're saying she has a cold."

"Smart girl," Dan said approvingly.

"But I've had horses with colds before. They never looked as bad as Star."

Dan reached in his bag and came out with a hypodermic and a plastic vial. "She's got a touch of bronchitis, too. Not too bad at this point. But you have to remember that horses are a lot like people in some respects. Different ones react to illness in different ways. Now, this lady—" he slapped Star's neck, and Cassie only belatedly realized that he was administering an injection "—is like some people when *they* get sick. She's feeling terribly, terribly sorry for herself." He removed the hypodermic from Star's neck, the job so skillfully done that the horse hadn't seemed to notice.

A big smile spread over Cassie's face. "You're right. Of course, you're right. Star's always had a tendency to sulk. Not that she isn't a good girl." She paused, then said, "What was the shot you gave her?"

"An antibiotic for the secondary infection. It ought to be repeated every day for the next week or so." Dan smiled inwardly. Daily visits wouldn't be at all irksome in this case, he thought. "I'll stop by—probably in the afternoons—and take care of it."

"You don't have to do that. Frankly, I can't afford so many house calls."

"That's okay," he began, meaning to invent some mythical discount rate for daily visits.

"No, it's not necessary," she insisted. "I've given shots to horses plenty of times before. I can come by the office later today and pick up some syringes and antibiotic."

Dan shrugged, then said reluctantly, "Okay. But you won't have to come to the office. I've got some extras in my bag. I'll leave them for you."

He came out of the stall and stood only a foot away from Cassie. Too close, rang the warning bells in her mind. She took a step backward, putting a little extra distance between them. "Anything else I should do for Star?"

"Keep the blanket on her. And you might give her a bran mash with her evening feed."

"Okay. Anything else?"

"One more thing. But it's not about Star." He looked down at Cassie, his eyes focused on her face.

Uh-oh! she thought. *Here comes trouble!*

What he said took her completely by surprise. "I owe you another apology, it seems."

"What for?"

"What I was thinking, earlier, about your stable. You're absolutely right. The place is safe. As weather-tight as most barns I've seen, and as danger free."

"Oh," she said and smiled.

He glanced around. "I guess I'm used to stables that are all prettied up for the owners who come to visit. Now I take a closer look, I can see that this place is perfectly sound. It's only the, uh, cosmetic aspects that're a little lacking. Sorry. Hope you don't mind me saying that."

"How could I mind? It's true. I wish I could fix it up—get some new fencing put in out front and give the whole place a coat of paint. As a matter of fact, every year I swear I'm going to get it done." She gave a little shrug. "But there's never quite enough money."

There was a touch of concern in Dan's voice. "The stable isn't doing well, then? I would have thought in the summer there'd be plenty of customers."

"There are. Lots of tourists like to go trail riding. And the kids love the pony rides. Then there are the boarders. That's year-round, of course."

"Then I don't understand why..."

"The money just seems to go for other things." She didn't feel she knew him well enough to tell him about one of the major drains on her profits. She rarely spoke of her "little hobby," as she called her efforts to rescue aging or ailing horses. People either thought she was silly or viewed her as some kind of plaster saint. But Cassie knew that she helped the animals for the satisfaction it gave her.

Determined to change the subject, she said, "By the way, are you going to be available tomorrow? The hauler's coming to take a bunch of the horses down to Banning to winter pasture. I always worry one of them'll get hurt while we're loading."

"I'll be in the office. I think I've got a pretty full schedule in the morning, but if there's an emergency, of course I'll come over." Gladly, he thought. And he realized how strangely his mind had been working this morning. Strange for him, anyway. He was still wishing he could make those daily house calls, for instance, when it was obvious that Cassie was perfectly capable of handling the simple injections required. And now his mind was racing, trying to come up with reasons why he shouldn't leave just yet . . . even though his job was done.

Just like a kid with a first crush, seeking excuses to hang around the object of his infatuation, he thought sarcastically. Only he was no kid. And his dealings with women had always been straightforward. When he met a woman who attracted him, he'd asked her out. She either accepted or she didn't. If she didn't, then that was that.

For a moment he thought of doing with Cassie what he would have done in the past. Suggest dinner. A movie. Whatever. See what she'd say.

Only he already knew what she'd say. No.

Knowing that, he ought to just walk away, as he would have with any other woman of his acquaintance. But he couldn't. Not this time. Whatever it was with him and Cassie McLean was different. The pull was too strong.

He glanced at the gray horse inside the stall, then said to Cassie, "The mare ought to feel a little better in a couple of hours. But if she doesn't eat by this evening, give me a call."

"I will. Thanks."

Dan picked up his bag. Cassie turned toward Star's stall and walked past him, careful not to get *too* close. Just having him around was disconcerting enough, without physical contact to add to her confusion.

She went into the stall, tossed the blanket over the mare and did up the straps. When she came out again, Dan was still standing in the aisle.

His continued presence wasn't really a surprise. As she'd bent to buckle Star's blanket, she had felt his gaze on her, warming her as effectively as the blanket did the mare.

Wherever did you get such a ridiculous notion, Cassie McLean? she asked herself. Gazes didn't warm people. She was being foolish.

She fell in step beside him as he walked toward the open doors. "Well, thanks again for coming out, Dan," she said brightly.

A few strides into the yard, he stopped to stamp his feet, shod in thin black leather loafers. "As you can see, I got myself a heavy jacket. But it looks like I'm going to need boots if I'm going to spend much time hanging out in cold barns."

"Get the kind with the fleece lining." Cassie extended one foot to show him her square-toed boots. "Like these. They're lots warmer."

"Thanks for the suggestion." With a trace of reluctance in his tone, he said, "Well, I guess I'd better be on my way."

Cassie hesitated. If she had any sense at all, she wouldn't say what she was about to say. But he had been awfully nice to come so quickly. And it was obvious he was feeling the cold. She said slowly, "If you don't have to go back to the office right away, how about a cup of coffee? I've got some made."

Dan grinned. "That'd hit the spot."

Blunder trotted behind them as they walked to the house and through the back door into the kitchen. It was a warm and cheery place, with a large oak table in the center. The room was papered with an old-fashioned flower print and copper pans hung on one wall.

Cassie stripped her gloves and jacket off, then got the coffeepot from the stove and filled two mugs. Dan removed his jacket and hung it over the back of one of the straight-backed kitchen chairs, then sat down. When Cassie put the mug in front of him, he cupped his hands around it, leaning forward to inhale the steam.

"How about a bear claw?" she asked. "I got them at the bakery yesterday, but they're still pretty fresh."

"Sounds great."

She took two of the pastries from a bread box on the counter. As she stuck them into the oven to warm, a loud wheeze came from the next room, followed by an undeniably human snore.

Dan's dark eyebrows arched inquiringly.

Cassie said calmly, "That must be Willie." She went to the swinging door that led out of the kitchen and pushed it open.

Dan leaned forward. The view from the kitchen showed an old man lying flat on his back on a chintz-covered couch. His mouth gaped open. First a whistle, then a snort came from the recumbent figure.

As Cassie let the door swing shut, Dan cast her a curious glance. "It's probably none of my business, but who's Willie?"

"He works for me . . . in the summertime." A quick glance at Dan's face told her that he found her explanation insufficient. "I found him sleeping it off in a stall this morning. I told

him to come into the house and get some coffee and clean up
a little. Looks like he decided he needed some more beauty
sleep."

"I see," Dan said, though he didn't really. He tried and
failed to think of any women of his acquaintance who would
have seemed so calm about an old man who looked like a
bum dozing on their couches. Cassie McLean, he was beginning to think, was not the average woman. At least, she
wasn't a type he'd met before. Cassie wasn't a *type* at all, he
mentally amended, but an individual and certainly one he
wanted to get to know better—*if* she'd let him.

He didn't fool himself into thinking that her offer of a cup
of coffee meant a change of heart. She'd have done the same
for anyone who had seemed affected by the winter chill. Her
hospitality to the old man sleeping in her living room was
proof.

He watched her as she moved around the kitchen. Now
that she had her jacket off, he was able to freshen his memories of her slim grace. Not as much as he would have liked,
though. The loose sweatshirt that had been underneath the
jacket was insufficiently revealing.

Dan concentrated on her face. Somewhere along the way,
she'd finger-combed her hair, getting rid of the piece of hay.
Her blue eyes were bright, her cheeks still flushed. Her lips
were naturally pink—full and soft looking. Highly kissable.

He swallowed, thinking about kissing her, about his mouth
coming down on hers, his tongue probing the sweetness he
knew he'd find within. But before he could even come close
to doing something like that, he'd have to find some way of
convincing her to let go of whatever objections she had to the
two of them getting to know each other on a friendlier footing. *Much* friendlier, if Dan had anything to say about it.

He looked at the wooden table in front of him. In the center was a sheaf of golden dried grasses in a thick white pot-

tery mug. The arrangement was attractive, yet simple and unpretentious. Like Cassie herself, he thought.

The only thing that wasn't simple about Cassie was that barrier she kept between them. At least, not in the sense of being easy to understand. He could challenge her on it, ask her why. But he sensed that would be a mistake, that it would force her to harden her position . . . to his ultimate cost. Better to use a ploy.

Dan Faraday, resorting to tactics? Give it up, Dan. The lady isn't interested. She made that clear, the first night. Came right out and said so.

Dan ignored the voice in his head. He was too busy considering how he could get Cassie to spend some more time in his company.

As she put a hot bear claw in front of him, he said, "Thanks," then cleared his throat. "I've been over at the Pizza Bar a couple of times this last week. I haven't seen you there."

Cassie sat down in the chair across from Dan's and reached for her mug. Her fingers tightened around it. "That's because I haven't been there."

He chuckled. "Oh, is that the reason?" He paused, then said casually, "A couple of people commented on the fact that you hadn't been around. They seemed surprised. Someone said you usually come in two or three nights a week."

"Usually, I do," she admitted noncommittally.

"Any particular reason you've stayed away?"

She straightened. "No, of course not. What reason could there be?" He couldn't have figured out that she was avoiding him. Could he? Oh yes, he could, she thought. Especially with her big-mouthed fellow Pinetoppers providing him with information.

He seemed to accept that she wasn't going to volunteer an explanation and said, "Anyway, we never did shoot any pool. How about a game tonight?"

Cassie stared down at her coffee cup. What was that Carly Simon song with the line about clouds in your coffee? Her coffee was clear; it was her mind that was foggy. She almost wanted to accept. "Well, I don't know," she equivocated. "I might be busy."

Dan leaned toward her across the table, his eyes fixed on her accusingly. "You know what, Cassie McLean? Anybody who didn't know any better might think you were afraid."

She wanted to lean back, away from him. But that would have proved he was right. She was scared silly—not of him, but of herself and her reaction to him. She squared her shoulders and scoffed, "Afraid! You've got to be kidding. What would I be afraid of?"

Dan's dark eyes were still fixed on her face. "Afraid I'd beat you at pool, of course."

A relieved laugh bubbled from her throat. "Now, that's really silly! I'm not afraid of anybody when it comes to pool."

"That's what I thought. So you'll play me a couple of games tonight?"

The challenge in his voice and her need not to let him know her real reason for staying away from the Pizza Bar combined to work devilry in Cassie. "Okay," she said briskly. "You're on."

4

IT WAS A FULL MINUTE and a half before Cassie began regretting her rash words. And by that time, it was too late. Dan had glanced at his watch, said he'd better get back to the office, thanked her for the coffee and the bear claw . . . and departed. She had a hunch that at least one of his reasons for leaving was so she wouldn't have a chance to change her mind.

She looked up as she heard a noise from the living room. Willie pushed open the swinging door, running a hand across his white-stubbled jaw. "I'm sorry, Cassie. I meant to get started on the stalls right away, but I didn't feel so good."

"It's okay, Willie. Why don't you sit down? I'll pour you some coffee." There was only a little left in the bottom of the pot. She poured it out for Willie. "I'll make some more. It'll just take a minute."

As she cleaned out the pot and refilled it with water, she considered what to do about Willie. A truly noble person would invite him to stay in the spare bedroom, she thought, which just went to show how noble *she* was. She simply couldn't have him sleeping in the house.

A possible solution occurred to her and she turned toward the old man. "If you don't have any place to stay tonight, I could put a cot in the tack room for you. I've got an electric heater I could put in there, too."

Willie smiled. "That'd be real nice, Cassie."

"But it couldn't be for more than a day or two," she cautioned. Judging by his former pattern, it would be several days at least before he went on another bender. "And you have to absolutely promise me you won't smoke in the barn."

"I won't." The little man wrapped his hands around his coffee mug. "You don't have to worry none. Anyhow, I'm thinking it's about time I took off for winter quarters." The glance he shot her was frankly calculating. "If I could find me a ride down the mountain, that is."

Cassie perked up. With luck, she might get rid of him tomorrow. "Maybe Fred Hanson will let you ride with him when he takes the horses down."

"Maybe," Willie said reluctantly. "He'll be going to Banning, though. I was kinda thinking about Palm Springs this year. Maybe work for some of those fancy people that live there."

Two roads led down opposite sides of the mountain, one to the glitzier desert resort towns, including Palm Springs, the other to the more prosaic area where Cassie's horses were pastured.

She wondered if Willie's choice of Palm Springs wasn't a mistake. The "fancy people" might not be inclined to let a seedy-looking old man do their odd jobs. But it was up to him. "I'll ask around," she promised. "Maybe someone's going to Palm Springs in the next day or two."

He swallowed a mouthful of coffee, then said earnestly, "I'm real sorry to leave you in the lurch, Cassie. But these winters up here just aren't good for old bones."

"I understand," she said. The truth was, she didn't need him in the winter and couldn't have afforded to pay him, anyway. "I know you always go down the mountain in the winter."

"That's right." Willie nodded vigorously. "That's what I do."

A BLUE HAZE of cigarette smoke was already wafting around the rafters by the time Cassie arrived at the Pizza Bar that evening. She was a little later than she had intended. After fixing dinner for Willie and getting him settled in the tack room for the night, it had taken her at least three times as long as usual to decide what to wear. By the time she finally settled on tan slacks and a russet-colored sweater with a boat neck and dolman sleeves, a heap of rejected garments lay on her bed.

She had gazed ruefully at the heap. Since when did she fret and stew over what she wore? Since Dan Faraday came to town, was the answer. And it was an answer Cassie didn't like one little bit.

Inside the Pizza Bar's front door she searched the room for Dan. She spotted him in the alcove near the back watching Jack Webley and Harry Greville, the owner of the Pizza Bar, play pool.

Amazingly, just as she spotted him, Dan seemed to sense her arrival. He looked up. His eyes met hers, and even across the whole length of the room, Cassie felt a little zing of connection. It wasn't what she wanted to feel, or even what she should be feeling. She was only here to play a little pool.

By the time she had taken off her jacket and hung it on the rack near the door, Dan reached her. He took her arm and smiled. "You made it! I was starting to wonder if you'd changed your mind."

As the minutes had ticked by and she still hadn't appeared, Dan began to worry, then to fret. Over a missed opportunity to play *pool* with a woman? Ridiculous, he had told himself. And that wasn't it, anyway. What bothered him was that if she failed to appear, it would be another statement of her refusal to get involved with him—even to let them get to know each other. Just another way of saying no.

Only he wasn't taking no for an answer. Some time during the day, he had silenced the voice that had pointed out that chasing a woman, the way he seemed to be hell-bent on chasing Cassie, was not Dan Faraday's style. That part of him was bound and gagged and stuffed in a closet somewhere. As far as Dan was concerned, it was full speed ahead.

Now Cassie was here. Her arm felt delicate yet strong under his hand. He wished they could be alone somewhere where he could discover more about the rest of her, touch her, kiss her. He imagined her blue eyes darkening with desire. Beneath her sweater he could see the outline of her small rounded breasts. He imagined them swelling with passion, the nipples hardening . . .

And he had to stop imagining or everyone in the room would know exactly what he had on his mind, he thought, feeling the tightening pull in his groin.

"How's Star doing?" he asked as he led her deeper into the room.

"It was just like you said. She started looking better a couple of hours after you left. This evening she ate up all her bran mash and then started in on her hay."

Dan nodded in satisfaction. "Good. Glad to hear it." He glanced toward the alcove in the back. Both pool tables were in use. "Looks like we'll have to postpone our game for a little while." Which was fine with him. The longer the pool tables were tied up, the longer he was assured of Cassie's company. "Can I buy you a beer?"

She narrowed her eyes. "Aha! The man's trying to get me to mess up my reflexes with alcohol. No thanks. I think I'll stick to Coke this evening."

"You're taking this match of ours awfully seriously, aren't you?"

"Sure. Aren't you?"

"That depends . . . on what we're betting on the match."

"A dollar," she said promptly.

"I was thinking of slightly higher stakes. Like dinner at the Pine Tree." The place he named was Pinetop's nicest restaurant. "Loser buys." It was the perfect bet as far as Dan was concerned. Either way, he won.

For a moment, Cassie wavered. Dinner at the Pine Tree sounded appealing. Good food. Good wine. Pleasant conversation. All preludes to danger if her companion was Dan Faraday. She said, "Sorry. That's too rich for my blood."

Dan gazed at her. For a second there, she'd looked as if she might agree. His terms were innocuous enough. It wasn't as if he'd suggested wagering a wild weekend—much as the thought appealed to him. But he wasn't actually surprised that she'd refused. And it wasn't just because she might have to pay if she lost the match; that was one thing he was certain of. Money had nothing to do with this.

Oh, well, he thought. So what if it hadn't worked? He'd known this wasn't going to be easy.

"What if I promised to lose?" he said lightly.

"No deal!" Her tone was indignant. "This match has got to be fair and square."

"Okay, okay." He held up his hands in laughing protest. "It was just a thought." It suddenly occurred to him that he must have hit the nail on the head this morning when he'd suggested she was afraid. Not of losing at pool, though. Afraid of him? No, that wasn't it, either. Afraid of herself? Not quite on, but close. He had it now. She was fearful of the attraction between them. But why? She was no fragile little miss, unable to deal with strong emotion. She must have her reasons. Try as he might, he couldn't think what they could be. But his intuition told him it was still too soon to just come right out and ask her.

He looked down at her. With a little luck—no, make that a *lot* of luck, considering the crowded room filled with people Cassie knew—they'd have some form of privacy, a chance to talk tonight. Maybe he'd pick up a clue or two.

Cassie pointed toward a corner. "I just spotted an empty table. Hadn't we better grab it?"

Dan nodded. "I'll get the drinks and meet you there."

His progress to the bar was slowed by the number of people greeting him and stopping to say a word or two. Pinetop was so different from the casual anonymity of L.A. He hadn't gotten used to it yet, and tonight, when he wanted to spend every possible moment with Cassie, it was a small irritation.

Predictably, a few of those who spoke to him were angling for free veterinary advice. "It sounds as if you'd better bring Wolf in," he said when a man had finished describing his dog's symptoms. "If he's scratching his ear a lot, it could be an infection."

Having finally gotten Cassie's Coke and a beer for himself from the bartender, he looked across the room. Cassie wasn't at the table she had pointed out. He spotted her sitting with a middle-aged couple. The woman, a flamboyant bleached blonde, seemed to be doing most of the talking while her balding companion quietly nursed a drink.

He should have realized that Cassie might want to join some of her friends. Just because he would have preferred sitting at a table alone with her didn't mean she felt the same.

He made his way over to the table. As he came up behind Cassie, he heard her say, "Thanks, Marj. That's great. I'll tell Willie."

Cassie was pleased. And relieved. Marjorie Simmons, who always knew everything about everyone, thought she could arrange a ride for Willie to Palm Springs with Jim Drexel, the editor/manager of the *Weekly Pinecone*, who was going down the mountain the following day. For Jim's sake, Cassie decided to try to get Willie to take a bath before he set off.

She looked up to see Dan standing next to her chair, then introduced him to Marj and Joe, explaining that the Simmonses owned and ran the bakery. She started to say, "That was one of their bear claws you had this morning," but, realizing what conclusion Marj would jump to, substituted, "Their stuff's terrific. You ought to try it."

"I will," Dan promised.

"Have a seat," Marj said with an expansive gesture.

Cassie looked questioningly at Dan. "We can only stay a minute. We're supposed to be playing pool."

"No free table," Marj said sensibly after glancing at the alcove. "You might as well light for a while."

So much for *any* hope of private conversation, Dan thought, trying to hide his frustration as he slid Cassie's Coke in front of her and sat down.

As Cassie had expected, with a newcomer at her mercy, Marj went into her well-known interrogation routine. Pinetop wisdom had it that in the event of the town experiencing a serious crime, Marj ought to be deputized to grill the suspect.

Within about two minutes, Cassie had learned that Dan had turned thirty-two last month, that he had never been married and that he had been born and raised in New York State, had gone to college there and to vet school in Pennsylvania.

"So what brought you out west, Doc?" Marj inquired.

Cassie watched him as he answered. His tone was casual, but she saw the slight tensing of his jaw. "A man I met while I was doing my residency offered me some work with a racing stable in L.A. For the past five years, I've been a racetrack vet."

"Oh? How come you decided to leave the track?" Marj asked.

Dan's face went bleak. His gaze was hooded, wary. Definitely something there, Cassie thought. Something painful he'd rather not talk about. She looked toward the alcove. Before Dan had to answer, she said brightly, "Hey, there's a pool table free. We'd better get it while we can." She stood, ending the conversation. "See you later."

She noted Dan's look of relief as he rose. But they had only taken a few steps away from the table when Marj called, "Cassie! Wait a minute! You won't forget the town meeting Monday night, will you?"

"Now, Marj. when did I ever miss a meeting?"

"Three years ago," Marj said promptly. "You had the flu."

Cassie chuckled. "You never forget anything, do you?"

"Of course not. It's my job to remember." She glanced at Dan. "You come, too, Doc."

"Thanks," he said with vague politeness. "Maybe I will." As he and Cassie walked toward the alcove, he asked, "What did she mean, about it being her job to remember?"

"Marjorie's the official town historian. She keeps records on everything that happens."

"Including your bout of flu, three years ago?"

"She was only kidding about that . . . I think. On the other hand, I bet she's right. I did have the flu that year."

"At least she puts her curiosity to good use." Dan grinned ruefully. "I thought she was going to get my whole life history out of me."

"Another couple of minutes and she would have." If she hadn't deflected Marj, she might have found out what was bothering Dan about his former work. Not her business, anyway, she reminded herself.

Dan said, "Town historian. Town meetings. People around here really get involved in the community, don't they?"

"Of course! We live here. It's our town." She paused to consider. "Actually, it's more than that. Pinetop's small enough that living here is kind of like having an extra-large extended family. Sometimes we fight, just like families do, but basically people help each other out."

"It sounds like something out of the last century."

"We're more up to date than you might think," she retorted. "You'd be surprised, for one thing, how many local businesses are fully computerized."

"Hold on. I wasn't criticizing," he said, noticing how quickly she leaped to the defense of Pinetop and its people.

They had reached the alcove. Both tables were free now, so Cassie and Dan were relatively alone. She said, "I'm not saying it's *all* good. There is a negative side."

"For instance?"

"You may not have noticed, but at least fifteen people watched us cross the room. Some of them are looking at us right now." She lowered her voice. "And all of them are . . . *thinking* things."

"What kind of things?"

She glanced toward the main part of the room, then back at Dan and said candidly, "My guess is that about half of them are laying odds that you'll never get anywhere with me."

"And the other half?"

"The other half's decided that you and I are already an item. They can hardly wait for tomorrow so they can spread the word to the people who weren't here tonight."

Dan stared down at her. She had thought he might laugh, or perhaps look annoyed. The one thing she was not prepared for was the gravity of his gaze. "One question, Cassie. Which half is right?"

Although he feared he already knew her answer, he was burning to hear what she would say. Literally burning, he realized. From the moment he'd first seen her, he had desired her. Every time he saw her, he only desired her more. And dammit, why? She was far from being the most beautiful woman he'd ever met. And, although she was pretty and nicely dressed, she certainly wasn't glamorous.

No, it was something else. He had sensed from the first that being with her would be . . .

He didn't know what it would be, exactly, but he did know he wanted her with an intensity that was unlike anything in his previous experience. And he knew she wanted him, too. It was in her eyes when she looked at him. And it was evident at the times when she *wouldn't* look at him. Like now.

She spoke lightly. Only because his senses were hyper-acute to everything about her could Dan detect the edge in her tone. "The first half, of course."

Might as well give her fair warning, he thought, let her know that he wasn't just going to leave it. Part of him cautioned against speaking his mind. But he chose to ignore it. His voice deepened, challenging her. "Are you so sure of that? I'm not. I agree with the folks who think something's going on between us."

Cassie lifted her gaze and looked fully into his eyes. For a long moment she felt as if she were drowning in pools of melting chocolate. Bitter. Sweet. A pleasure beyond pleasure, yet pulling her into a vortex of emotion she was unwilling to experience, unless it could last.

Keep it light, Cassie! She said brightly, "I sure hope you play pool the same way you pick sides. You're way off base, Dan."

One of his eyebrows arched. "Am I?"

His eyes held hers. Cassie's head spun and her heart rattled alarmingly in her chest. Finally she wrenched her gaze away and turned toward the alcove. In a voice that emerged too high-pitched, she cried, "Well, come on, Dan. Let's play some pool. Best three out of five?"

THEIR FIRST GAME of eight ball was, in Cassie's opinion, one of the worst ever to disgrace the Pizza Bar. Dan had told her he hadn't played in years, so he had an excuse. But it was plain ridiculous that Cassie McLean, Pinetop's unofficial pool champion, should fumble shots a child of two should have been able to make.

Her failings were caused by an inability to concentrate. Dan had let her know in no uncertain terms that he wasn't going to back off just because she wanted him to. *Wanted* him to? Was that really the truth? Wasn't she secretly delighted—*thrilled*—that he'd made his interest so unequivocally plain? Maybe so, but her common sense and instinct for self-preservation were absolutely determined not to let her get involved with a man whose presence in her life would be only temporary.

Unfortunately neither the weak nor the strong parts of Cassie were playing decent pool tonight. Her wits were scattered; her hand-eye coordination was a wreck.

Toward the end of the first game, she pulled herself together enough to eke out a narrow victory. Dan seemed unfazed by his defeat. "I told you I was rusty," he said casually.

It wouldn't do to let him see how embarrassed she was by her poor performance, she decided. "Maybe I should have agreed to higher stakes, after all."

"It's not too late to play for that dinner."

Still tempting. Still dangerous. She shook her head. "Nope. It wouldn't be fair to take advantage of you."

His grin was wicked, investing her words with a double meaning she hadn't intended. "I wouldn't complain a bit."

"Your break," Cassie said tersely.

To her humiliation, Dan easily won the second game. "I thought it'd come back pretty fast," he said.

"You just got lucky," she retorted.

But he won the next game, too. And something strange happened to Cassie. She began to see their match as a symbol of the battle that had begun the instant they'd met and had intensified each time she'd seen him. It wasn't a battle between him and her, exactly. It was more a battle within herself, but with Dan's forces allied with the part of her that wanted to give in to the strong attraction between them. On the opposing side, battling alone, was the sensible Cassie who knew that no good could come of an involvement with a man who was bound to decamp in a few weeks or a few months.

Not that she intended, if she lost the match, to surrender. No way. But she had the strange feeling that if she lost to him, her defenses would be breached, making it that much more difficult to resist.

She won the next game, evening the score. Dan paused for a swallow of his beer, and Cassie was so tense that she blurted, "No stalling, now. Your break."

As he racked the balls, Jack and Mary Jo drifted into the alcove. "Who's winning?" Jack asked with interest.

"We're tied two to two," Cassie admitted reluctantly. "We're about to play the tiebreaker."

"Well, I'll be damned." Jack grinned at Dan. "It's about time somebody put her in her place, Doc. Go to it!"

"I haven't won yet," Dan warned.

"You've got to," Jack insisted. "There's a whole lot at stake here. The honor of us menfolk, for one."

With that, Mary Jo chimed in, "You'd better beat him, Cassie. You're fighting for the superiority of women, now."

Jack snorted. "Superiority, huh! Equality...*maybe*." Mary Jo punched him on the arm.

People at nearby tables must have overheard the exchange, because nearly a dozen men and women crowded into the alcove to watch what Jack was now proclaiming a decisive skirmish in the battle of the sexes. Side wagers were made and Cassie winced to hear Sandra Maxwell, the town's resident beautician, bet twenty dollars on her. Now she *had* to win—not just for herself, but for the women of Pinetop.

"And for women everywhere," she murmured to herself.

Dan gave her a startled look. "What?"

"Nothing."

Dan scratched on the break, scattering the balls but failing to put any of them away. Cassie moved up to the table and made a shot that neatly dropped number seven into a pocket. Feminine cheers and masculine groans filled the alcove. Her next shots were just as good. Ball after ball went where she intended.

She had him, she thought triumphantly. One more critical shot to make and she'd be able to close him out, winning the game without ever having to give up control.

A hush fell as Cassie bent over the table and lined up her cue. A clean tap. She held her breath and ball number six went rolling . . . to stop just short of the corner pocket.

She exhaled a sigh that was lost in the cheers of the male contingent.

Dan rosined his cue and stepped up to the table, eyeing the placement of the balls like a general surveying hostile terrain. He made his first shot. Then another and another.

For his fourth, he leaned over the table only a couple of feet in front of where Cassie stood. She should have been watching his play, but her attention was riveted by the way his jeans hugged his firm buttocks. Good grief, the man had a great body, she thought. Not bulging with overdeveloped muscles, but lean and strong.

Dan walked to the other side of the table, made his fifth shot, then returned to where she was standing. The devil got into Cassie. She wasn't even thinking about the consequences of the game. It was just that bent over, he made such a tempting target. And no one was watching her; all eyes were on the table as he lined up his cue.

He drew it back. Cassie's hand, guided by the imp from hell that had taken possession of her, moved forward, slapped onto his right buttock and briefly squeezed.

Dan jerked. His shot went awry, slamming into the bumper inches from the pocket.

"Aw, man," Jack complained. "You should have made that one easy."

Dan turned slowly to face Cassie.

She tried to assume a mask of innocence. Oh, Lordy! Why had she done it? He'd be furious. He'd tell everyone she'd interfered with his shot. And exactly how.

But his eyes were sparkling with mischief. "Lucky for you I blew it."

"Wasn't it?" She spoke blandly, but her palm still tingled from the feel of rock-hard muscle.

He bent and spoke quietly, so only she could hear him. "Better look out. I'll pay you back for that if I get the chance."

"You won't. I'll make sure of that."

The rest of the game was super slow, because Cassie had a new element to factor into her choice of angles for each shot— keeping out of Dan's reach.

Onlookers gazed at her in astonishment as she bent herself into positions a contortionist would have envied, just to keep her distance from Dan. The men, who normally would have been happy to point out the flaws in her approach, were pleased to see her make things difficult for herself; the women acknowledged Cassie as their undisputed superior when it came to pool. As a result, she was allowed her crazy positions without comment—except from Dan, whose commentary was silent. Three times she glanced at him to see him mouthing, "I'll get you," or lifting his dark brows significantly.

Regardless, she made her shots. Sheer determination and a generous portion of luck were on her side. Finally, her last ball dropped into the pocket to delighted cries and applause from the women, moans of disgust from the men.

Dan threw his hands in the air. "She's a pool hustler. I should have known."

Money changed hands. Dan waved to the one waiter, Harry Greville's nephew, who occasionally circulated through the Pizza Bar. "A round for everybody. On me," Dan said.

He looked toward Cassie. She stood on the open side of the alcove with Mary Jo and Sandra Maxwell. She said something he couldn't hear, then eased away from the other two women and took a backward step and then another into the main room.

"That little rat!" he muttered. He was half-amused, half-annoyed. His hopes for the evening as a time to get to talk to Cassie, to learn more about her, had dissolved long since. That would have to wait, though not for long, if he had anything to say about it. But he certainly wasn't going to just let her slip away. He reached into his pocket, then pressed several folded bills into Jack's hand. "See to it that everybody gets what they want, will you, Jack?"

"Sure. But where are you going, Doc?"

"I have to make sure someone gets what she deserves."

He saw that by now Cassie was almost halfway to the front door. In another minute, she'd have grabbed her jacket and hurried outside. He glanced behind him at a door in the alcove. It had better be the back way out, he thought.

Cassie exhaled into the chill night air. Dan hadn't even noticed her getaway, yet as far as she was concerned, it was a necessary evasive tactic. He might not have managed to retaliate while the match was still under way, but she was under no illusion that he intended to let the matter drop.

She shoved her hands into the pockets of her jacket. She had driven tonight, and her pickup truck was parked in the lot beside the Pizza Bar. She turned around the corner of the building . . . and gasped.

A tall figure leaned against the driver's side door of her truck, his arms in shirtsleeves crossed over his chest. By the time she got closer, she had managed to hide her surprise. She said calmly, "You must be a little chilly without a jacket."

"Freezing," Dan agreed amiably. "I thought maybe you could warm me up a little. You owe it to me, you know."

"It's not my fault if you're fool enough to come out like that."

"No, but it is your fault that I lost the game. That little maneuver of yours was pretty cute."

"All's fair in—" she began, then broke off. This was neither love nor war, was it? Except that right now it seemed to be a little of both.

"Go ahead. Finish what you were going to say."

She shrugged. "You know how that saying ends. Now would you mind stepping aside? I need to get home. The trailer's coming early tomorrow."

"In a minute." It was pretty dumb of him to come charging outside, Dan thought, but worth it, even if he caught pneumonia. At least, he *hoped* it would turn out to be worth it. "I told you I was going to pay you back, Cassie."

He stood, looking solidly immovable—a pretty feat for a man who was shivering—and blocked the door to her truck. Laying hands on him in an attempt to shift him was out of the question. Her palm still felt the imprint of that brief squeeze she'd given him. Maybe if she played his game, didn't struggle . . .

She let out an exaggerated sigh. If he wanted to squeeze her where she'd squeezed him, she supposed she could endure it. The trick would be not to enjoy it too much. "Oh, all right," she said. "Go ahead. Let's get it over with, so I can get out of here." She turned her back on him, steeling herself for the touch of his hand on her bottom.

But when she felt both his hands, it was not on her behind, after all. Instead, his long fingers molded her shoulders. "That's very... acquiescent of you," he said, with laughter in his voice. "Not like you at all. But that wasn't what I had in mind."

He turned her to face him, then put one hand behind her head, sliding his fingers through her hair. His other arm encircled her waist. His breath made a cloud in the air as he bent toward her, a cloud that mingled with the cloud of her own breathing. She meant to say, "No, Dan," and turn her head away. But she couldn't. She was mesmerized. His lips moved closer, then closer still.

His mouth was cool, but not cold as it met hers. And there was nothing even slightly chilly about the way he kissed her. His lips took slow, thorough possession of hers, as if he had all the time in the world and meant to use it kissing her.

Nor was her response the cool one she'd have liked it to be. Her lips parted, though she hadn't meant them to. The tip of his tongue probed tentatively, then, with the same sweet leisureliness, filled her mouth.

Heat flowed through her. As he tasted and teased her with his tongue, the attraction she had felt from the very first intensified a thousandfold. Desire blossomed in her lower body, and she clung to him, kissing him back through what felt like an eternity of pleasure and mounting passion.

She felt his erection swelling against her lower body. Intoxicating though the sensation was, it broke the spell. She wasn't being fair to Dan, kissing him like that when she had no intention of letting him share her bed.

She pulled back against his arm, and he let her go. Her lips trembled, her heart pounded, and her knees felt rubbery. *Keep it light, Cassie.* She said brightly, "Well, I guess we're even-steven."

"I'd say so," Dan agreed.

"Good. I'll sleep much better tonight, knowing that."

He lifted one quizzical brow. "Will you? I won't."

She had no answer to that one. She had a hunch that slumber would come slowly to her, too. "Just one thing, Dan. Since we're even up, you won't find it necessary to do that again, will you." She made it a statement, not a question.

He stared at her for a moment, then threw back his head. The still cold night echoed with his laughter. "You know the answer to that one already, Cassie. Don't pretend you don't. But it'll do for now." He tipped her a salute, then moved out of her way. "Thanks for the *game*." He invested the word with a wealth of meanings. "Good night."

It was several seconds before Cassie could pull herself together enough to climb into her truck, turn the ignition and drive away.

Dan watched her truck's taillights as she drove out of the parking lot, then he wheeled and headed for the Pizza Bar. He plunged through the back door of the building, not caring a bit that he had goosebumps all over his body. It was as he'd thought—hoped—it would be when he kissed her. Fire had met fire. The riches of passion he had suspected lived in her slender body were all there . . . and more.

Best of all, he knew from her response that she wanted him as much as he wanted her, even if she wasn't quite ready to admit it yet.

When was he going to see her again? How soon? A thought struck him, and he was thoroughly ashamed of himself. For an instant he had found himself hoping that something would happen while her horses were being loaded tomorrow, nothing serious, of course, just some little thing that would require her friendly neighborhood vet to make another house call.

5

IT WAS STILL HALF DARK when a big blue horse van with Hanson's Hauling lettered on the side pulled up in the yard. The driver, a lean man whose baseball cap hid a scarcity of hair, stepped out of the cab.

"Morning, Fred." Cassie handed him a steaming mug of coffee.

"Morning, Cassie. Thanks. This hits the spot." Fred buried his long nose in the mug.

"Would you like to come in and warm up for a minute?"

Fred shook his head. "Thanks, but we'd better get on with it."

Cassie hid a smile. Twice each year, when Fred drove her horses down the mountain and again when he brought them back in the spring, they went through the same ritual. Cassie would invite Fred in, and he would decline, claiming the need to hurry. Then, without seeming to notice any contradiction, he would engage her in a leisurely conversation.

He did so now, telling Cassie all about his daughter who was studying to be a C.P.A. and his son's triumphs as a high school football star.

Then he said, "Say, Cassie. I got a tip for you. Might be worth your while to go to Art's this week."

Art's A-1 Weekly Auction, down the mountain near Banning, was an institution. Every Sunday afternoon, goats, pigs and horses were auctioned off. Cassie had bought several of her rental horses at Art's. "Really? Something interesting going on sale?"

Fred looked sly. "Let's just say that I got an order to pick up two at John Manners's place and take 'em to Art's on Saturday."

"*Really!*" She would definitely have to go. Her two most reliable and willing animals, Star and King, had both been broken and trained by Manners. The man seemed to have a magic touch with horses. She had already decided she needed one or two more horses for next season, but had planned to wait until later in the year. She couldn't pass up a chance at a Manners-trained animal, though.

Going to the auction presented a problem, she realized. Wise horse buyers always had a veterinarian check the animal's health and condition before a purchase was made. In the past Doc Anderson had always gone with her to the auctions.

So what was the problem? she asked herself. There was a vet in town, and she had the feeling he wouldn't object to a trip down the mountain in her company.

The problem was that the mere thought of spending that much time with Dan made her stomach jump and her nerves flutter in anticipation. That kiss . . . It had let loose hungers she had thought herself well able to control. Sleep had been slow to come the night before. As she lay there, restless and tossing, her imagination had provided sensual recollections of Dan's mouth on hers, his arms wrapped around her, his body hard and urgent with desire.

Even now, the memory stirred her. She shifted uncomfortably and said, "Thanks, Fred. I think I'll try to go."

A noise from the stable made her turn. Willie came out the half-open door, rubbing sleep from his eyes. "I slept real good, Cassie," the old man said. "That cot you set up for me was real comfortable."

"I'm glad to hear it," Cassie said. "I've got good news for you, Willie. A ride down to Palm Springs this afternoon."

DAN SAT BEHIND THE DESK in the office he was temporarily occupying. In addition to the office, the building also contained a reception area, two treatment rooms, a spotless surgery and a small kennel facility. He had been pleasantly surprised to find how well equipped and up-to-date the place was.

There was a soft tap on the door. He called, "Come in." His receptionist, Ellen Rogers, stuck her head in. "Ready to get started, Doc?"

Dan stood. "Might as well. Who's first?"

"Mrs. Carmichael." Ellen seemed to be having some sort of problem, Dan noticed. Despite obvious efforts to control it, her mouth was twitching. "She's brought her—" Ellen choked "—her cat in for a checkup."

Dan regarded Ellen with suspicion. "Okay. What is there I ought to know about Mrs. Carmichael?"

"Not about her. It's her cat." Ellen's efforts at control broke down, and she dissolved into laughter.

Dan drummed his fingers on the desk. "Okay. What's the story on Mrs. Carmichael's cat?"

"You'll see."

"Now, Ellen, don't you think you ought to—" He broke off as the phone on his desk jingled, the lit button indicating his private line. For one crazy moment, he fantasized that it was Cassie calling to tell him she couldn't stand it a moment longer, that their kiss had awakened a need that demanded immediate fulfillment.

Nuts, Faraday. You're going nuts! He was the one suffering acute desire. As he had predicted, he hadn't slept worth a damn last night.

Cassie was a witch. That was the only explanation he could think of. She had cast a spell that had turned him into a teenager again, at least as far as his body's urges were concerned. Yet there was nothing boyish about his certainty that they were destined to come together in a joyous union. If only he could make her see . . .

He said to Ellen, "I'll take this call. Tell Mrs. Carmichael I'll be just a minute."

He picked up the phone to hear a hearty masculine voice say, "Hello, there, Faraday. It's Doc Anderson. Hope I'm not disturbing you. I thought I might catch you before you got started for the day."

"Your timing was perfect," Dan said. The day they had met to discuss Dan temporarily taking over the practice, he had immediately liked the older man.

"The truth is," said the genial voice, "I was just checking to see how you're doing. You settling in all right?"

"Just fine."

"How are you liking the practice so far? I know it's not what you're used to."

"Actually I'm kind of enjoying it," Dan said and discovered that he meant it. It hadn't been as difficult as he'd feared to refresh his knowledge of small animal treatment and bring it up-to-date. He'd been doing a lot of reading, not only texts but the journals that detailed recent advances in veterinary medicine.

"Pinetop is really a nice little town," Doc Anderson said fondly. "I never expected this damned chest of mine to drive me away." He sighed, then said briskly, "Well, that's neither here nor there. I guess I couldn't resist calling to check on you, Faraday. Forgive an old man's nosiness."

"There's nothing to forgive," Dan said warmly. "Naturally you'd want to know how your substitute is doing. You haven't found a buyer for the practice yet?"

"Not one I'd consider selling to. It has to be the right person. Someone who'll fit into Pinetop, understand the animals . . . and the people." Doc Anderson fell silent for a moment. "You haven't changed your mind, I don't suppose?"

"About buying the practice?" Anderson had made the offer near the end of their first and only meeting. "No, I haven't."

Doc Anderson said hesitantly, "You know, if the problem is financial, we could work things out."

Dan almost chuckled in the older man's ear. Finances were the least of his worries. For the past five years, he had made excellent money, and because he'd had the use of the track's superb veterinary facilities, it hadn't been necessary to set up an office of his own. The result was that he'd had enough money left over to invest in this and that. A smart broker and a lot of luck had made him one of the fortunate few. If he never worked another day in his life, he wouldn't starve. "No, it's not the money," he said. "As I told you before, I'm not the right man for this practice. I'm a racehorse vet."

And he would be a racehorse vet again, he thought. Surely, Owen Winwood couldn't keep him blacklisted forever. Sooner or later the other owners and trainers would see the man for what he was and realize that Dan couldn't have done what Winwood had accused him of.

Thinking of what had happened to him reminded Dan that he should make an appearance at the races in Los Angeles. He couldn't afford to let people think he'd disappeared. Next Sunday he'd go, he decided as he heard Doc Anderson say, "Sorry you feel that way, Faraday. If you should change your mind..."

"Thanks. But I'm afraid I won't."

"Well, I guess I'd better let you go." Doc Anderson chuckled. "By the way, have you seen Mrs. Carmichael's Tiger yet? It seems to me he was about due for a checkup."

"He's my first patient this morning. Why? What's the matter with him?"

Doc Anderson sounded just like Ellen, as if he were having a lot of trouble restraining laughter. "You'll see, Faraday.
You'll see."

Dan hung up, wondering what could be the big deal about
Mrs. Carmichael's cat. Nothing he couldn't handle, he was
certain. After all, he was accustomed to dealing with half a
ton of highly strung Thoroughbred. What trouble could he
have with a tiny little pussycat?

Only tiny was the wrong word for Tiger, he discovered
minutes later. Mrs. Carmichael, a thin, frail-looking woman
in late middle age, entered the treatment room lugging a cat
carrier. As Dan took it from her and hoisted it onto the
stainless steel examining table, he was astonished by its
weight.

He offered a few pleasantries, then unlocked the door of
the carrier and reached a hand inside. Daggerlike fangs
pierced the fleshy part of his thumb. Dan and Tiger let out
simultaneous yells. Dan slammed the carrier door shut. From
inside, Tiger glared at him, mad-eyed and menacing.

"Oh, dear. Did he bite you?" Mrs. Carmichael twittered.
"I'm so sorry." She peered at the carrier and said mildly, "Bad
cat."

Dan squeezed his thumb, then wiped the blood on a tis-
sue, thinking wistfully of antiseptic and Band-Aids. Later.
First, he had to deal with the cat. Before initiating a second
encounter, he found a pair of heavy leather gloves in a drawer
and slipped them on, then cautiously opened the cage door
and reached inside. Tiger spat and raked claws across the
back of Dan's left glove. No damage. The glove did the trick.
That fixes you, sucker, he thought.

He grasped the cat firmly around the middle and drew
Tiger out of the carrier. With a yowl, an enormous calico blur
shot out of Dan's hands, landed on the examination table,

then bounded to the top of a low cabinet. There the cat paused to glare malevolently at Dan.

"Oh, dear, you let him get away," Mrs. Carmichael pointed out.

Dan gritted his teeth. "Yes, I guess I did."

He walked slowly toward the cat. But Tiger, recognizing the enemy's advance, crouched, then sprang straight up in the air, defying gravity. From the top of an eight-foot, white metal cabinet, the cat growled and hissed.

"Oh, dear, he's up so high," Mrs. Carmichael said with concern. "I hope he doesn't fall."

Dan's mental stream of profanities could have blistered the paint off the walls. The knock on the door seemed to him the sweetest sound he'd ever heard. "Come in, Ellen," he called.

She pushed open the door. "Sorry to bother you, Doc, but Cassie McLean's on the phone. One of her horses was slightly injured in loading. She wondered if you could stop by her place sometime today."

Dan glanced at the yowling, spitting cat on top of the cabinet. "Injured! Good heavens! I'd better take a look at it right away."

Ellen took in the scene at a glance. In a bland voice, she said, "Cassie said it's not an emergency."

Dan scowled at his pleasant, efficient receptionist. "But she could be wrong. Who knows? The poor animal could bleed to death." He turned to Mrs. Carmichael. "I'm sure you understand why I'll have to postpone examining Tiger."

"Of course." Mrs. Carmichael sounded resigned. "You run along and take a look at the poor horse. I'll make another appointment."

Dan said, "Ellen, will you help Mrs. Carmichael get her cat down?" Served her right, he thought, for saying it wasn't an emergency.

"Oh, he'll come down the minute you leave," Mrs. Carmichael said. "It was always that way when Doc Anderson was called out on an emergency during one of our appointments. Goodness! When I think of the number of emergencies you vets have to deal with . . . Why, every time Tiger and I come here, it's something."

Dan said blandly, "Yes, there are often surprises in this line of work."

TWENTY MINUTES LATER Dan took a small and practically unnecessary stitch in Buster's right rear fetlock. Just after being loaded, Cassie had explained, the horse had lashed out with his hind feet. One leg had connected with the edge of the trailer. "That's it, then," he said to Cassie. "There's a little bruising, and he'll be sore for a day or two, but there's not much damage."

"That's what I thought," Cassie said. She untied Buster's rope from the hitching post. The first van load of horses had gone down the mountain, without Buster. And the brown horse wouldn't be making the second trip, either. She wanted him where she could keep an eye on him until he was fully healed. She said, "Dan, I really appreciate your coming right over, but I told Ellen it wasn't an emergency. I mean, I don't want you thinking that I expect you to rush over here for every little thing."

"I'm happy to come over anytime, Cassie," he said meaningfully.

He looked at her and a nearly palpable current flowed between them. How was she supposed to go on resisting the man when mere eye contact conjured up an ache of longing? she wondered. But did she even *want* to resist him anymore?

Of course she did, she insisted silently. *Leaving. Temporary. Short-term.* She recalled all the proper words, but for some reason the reminders had lost their power.

She toyed with the end of Buster's lead rope, conscious that she might be taking a step in a direction she oughtn't to go. "I was wondering if I could ask you a favor, Dan."

"Sure."

"There's an auction on Sunday. Down near Banning. I want to bid on a couple of horses. Doc Anderson always went with me to the sales to check the animals I was interested in. I'll pay your regular fee, of course."

Dan hesitated. When he came to Pinetop, he had promised himself that he wouldn't lose touch with the racing world. Currently they were running at the Santa Theresita track. He'd decided only that morning to drive down to L.A. on Sunday, make his presence felt, face down Owen Winwood, if necessary. Most of all he intended to show those who had believed the nasty tales about him that he hadn't slunk away like a whipped hound with its tail between its legs.

But the opportunity to spend most of a day with Cassie was too good to pass up. There would be other racing days.

"I was planning to go to L.A.," he said. "But it's okay. I can postpone that until another time."

"I wouldn't want to inconvenience you," she said. Obviously he still had ties in Los Angeles. A woman? There was no particular reason for her to think that was his reason for visiting the city. Then again, there was no reason for her to think it wasn't. And why should it matter? She wasn't going to get involved with him anyway. Was she?

"It's no problem," Dan insisted. "Just a bit of business. I can take care of it some other time."

"You're sure?"

"Absolutely positive," he said firmly. And then he had an idea. *Brilliant, Faraday. Brilliant!* "But there's one condition."

"What's that?

"That you go out with me on Saturday night."

She frowned, but the frown didn't touch her eyes. If anything she looked as if she were staring temptation in the face and having trouble saying no.

"That's not fair," she said.

"Why not? Naturally I'll waive my fee for going to the sale." Briefly he wondered what such a fee would be. He had gone to sales of racehorses and the going rate for his attendance was five hundred dollars and up. He couldn't imagine Doc Anderson had charged Cassie a tenth of that amount. "Is it a deal?"

"Well . . ." Cassie hesitated. She was standing at the edge of a precipice. An afternoon at an auction was a bit dangerous in itself, but an actual date . . .

At the very edge of the cliff, she dug in her toes. She'd agree to his deal, she decided, but with a twist. "Okay. You're on."

A big grin spread over Dan's face. He hadn't expected her to agree that easily. It meant she must be weakening, must be getting ready to admit there was something special between them. "Great! Seven o'clock okay?"

"Seven o'clock's fine. Only let's not go out. Why don't you come over here?"

"To the stable?" he asked, his suspicions instantly aroused. He could just imagine her planning a fun evening of stall cleaning, in order to keep him at arm's length.

"Of course not. To my house is what I meant."

Dan was startled. An evening *in*? Alone? An even deeper and darker suspicion crept over him. He'd been hoping for a turnaround in her attitude, but this was too sudden and complete to be real. He decided to play along. Deliberately lowering his voice to a silken caress, he said, "That sounds wonderful, Cassie. Wonderful." He allowed himself a hint of hesitation, just to see how far she'd go. "If you're sure you wouldn't rather go out somewhere?"

She said, much too promptly in Dan's estimation, "Of course I'm sure."

Dan said goodbye, then turned toward his van. The little devil! She planned to have a surprise waiting for him on Saturday night; he was certain of it. But what she didn't know was that whatever she had planned would be okay with him, assuming he got to spend some time with her. She might be playing havoc with his hormones, but he still didn't expect her to leap blithely into bed with him, just because his body wished she would.

As he unlocked the door of his van, he glanced back toward the stable. Cassie had disappeared.

IN THE TACK ROOM Cassie was trying to convince herself that the trick she'd played on Dan was an amusing joke, nothing more. But it wasn't like her to play silly games, which was exactly what she'd just done.

The last refuge of the truly desperate? That thought had the somber ring of truth. For some reason it was no longer possible for her to simply face Dan and tell him no . . . and mean it. Therefore, all she had left was to tease and play, twist and evade.

It *was* funny. She could hardly wait to see Dan's face when he showed up on Saturday night.

"Ha, ha," she said experimentally, then frowned. She'd have to go through with her plans now. She was committed. Or she ought to *be* committed. At the moment she wasn't sure which.

6

AT LEAST A DOZEN VEHICLES stood outside Cassie's house when Dan pulled into the stable yard on Saturday night. So safety in numbers was her ploy. Resourceful lady, he thought with a tinge of reluctant admiration.

As he parked his van, a pickup truck, larger than Cassie's, drove into the yard and stopped. Its doors opened. Jack Webley's voice floated across the frosty air. "Aw, come on, Mary Jo. Don't be that way."

The blonde alighted from the truck, flipping her ponytail back over the shoulder of her heavy jacket. "Don't be *what* way? I didn't do a thing."

"That's it. That's what I mean," said Jack. "You won't *do* anything. You won't say yes, you won't say no. Just leave a man hanging," he grumbled.

A kindred spirit, Dan thought dryly. Another man with woman trouble. He cleared his throat loudly. Jack and Mary Jo turned toward him. "Why, there's Doc. Hi, Doc!" the blonde said brightly.

Jack's greeting was less enthusiastic. He muttered something, and the three of them advanced toward the house together.

When Cassie opened the door, she seemed to be having trouble meeting his eyes. Was she afraid he might be angry because she had, in effect, brought half of Pinetop along on their date? He might have been annoyed, if he hadn't guessed well in advance that she had some trick in mind.

Without looking directly at Dan, Cassie beckoned the three of them into a short hall that opened on a living room crowded with people. All of the mountain town's younger set and some older people as well, were crammed into the room. Bowls of chips, vegetable plates, and dips were placed here and there. Most of the guests held either a beer or a soft drink can. Jack and Mary Jo, after a few words with their hostess, went on past to mingle with the crowd.

Dan looked down at Cassie and said ingenuously, "A party! Gee, this is great!"

For the first time she looked directly at his face. Her eyes narrowed. "You don't seem to be very surprised."

"I'm not. I figured you must have something like this up your sleeve. I just didn't know exactly what it would turn out to be."

Beyond, only a few feet away, people were laughing and talking, but the little space near the door seemed to be encapsulated in a temporary bubble of privacy. Dan's gaze lingered on her slim figure. She was clad in crisp jeans and a sage-green turtleneck sweater. He had never realized before what a partiality he had for that particular shade of green. Nor had it ever occurred to him that he could actually envy a garment its close contact with a human form. He imagined his hands and mouth where the sweater was, molding her breast, caressing her throat.

He lowered his voice to a husky murmur. "Nice sweater, Cassie."

A faint flush climbed her cheeks and Dan delighted to see two points thrust against the wool of her sweater. If he could make her nipples harden just by looking at her, talking to her, what would happen if they were alone together, naked skin sliding against naked skin, hands and mouths free to pleasure each other as he knew they could?

He felt himself begin to harden at the thought and purposefully brought to mind the least sexy image he could think of. It turned out to be Tiger glaring wildly at him. The remembered pain in his thumb, plus the realization that he would have to deal with the beast again before too long, effectively decreased his tumescence.

Cassie, he noticed, had hunched her shoulders slightly to hide the evidence of his effect on her.

He slipped off his jacket and hung it on a coat tree that stood near the door, "Okay," he said. "Let's party."

A few steps and they were in the middle of it. "Hey, Doc," people called. "How you doin', Doc?"

Cassie spent the next few minutes introducing Dan to the few Pinetoppers present he had not yet met. She was glad he wasn't furious at her for the trick she'd played on him, but less glad that he also seemed completely undeterred. Why had she thought that throwing up a wall of people between them would defeat him? And why should he feel defeated, for that matter, when her own body clearly betrayed her weakness where he was concerned?

She glanced up at his face as he greeted a couple of Pizza Bar regulars he obviously knew fairly well. He looked and acted as if he was settling in to have a good time. Smiling and at ease, he exchanged hellos and casual banter.

Was it possible that in time he'd come to see the merits of this place and its people? Enough that he might consider staying permanently?

Don't go wishful thinking, Cassie, she instructed herself. Dan had neither said nor done a single thing to give her hope. But, oh, how nice it would be if he *were* staying. She could stop fighting her attraction to him and go with the flow . . . which, in this case, she knew full well, meant directly into Dan Faraday's arms and, not too long thereafter, into bed.

She glanced at Dan. Clem Jones from the barber shop had pulled him into conversation. She heard Clem say, "Hey, Doc, I was talking to Doc Anderson the other day and . . ."

The rest was lost as Alison Levitt, a dark-haired woman with a dramatic silver streak winging away from her temple, touched Cassie's arm. "Say, Cass," she said, "when am I going to get your latest batch of stuff? The walls at the gallery are looking pretty empty."

By the time Cassie had finished making arrangements with Alison, Dan had moved on, into a group that included Jack and Mary Jo. She noticed that Dan didn't have a drink. Fine hostess she was. She'd neither gotten him anything nor invited him to help himself from the kitchen.

She turned in that direction. A couple of steps brought her next to Clem Jones, whose own thinning, disheveled locks were a poor advertisement of his skill at cutting and shaping the hair of Pinetop's males. "Clem, I heard you mention Doc Anderson a little while ago. Have you talked to him? How's he doing?"

"Doing just fine, Cassie," Clem said with a smile. "I was down the mountain a couple of days ago and stopped in. Doc's got a nice little house. Chest is doing fine. Only thing bothering him is that he wants to get the practice sold. Get it all wrapped up, I guess, so he don't have to worry about it no more."

Cassie frowned. Added to her affection for Doc Anderson was a deeply personal curiosity. "Oh? Is anybody interested in buying?"

"Nobody Doc wants to sell to. Not yet." Clem leaned closer. "Just between you and me, Cassie, Doc Anderson wishes like anything that Doc Faraday'd buy it. Offered it to him a couple of times, he said, but Doc Faraday keeps saying no."

Okay. That's it. End of wishful thinking time! She couldn't have gotten a clearer message about the odds on Dan deciding to stay in Pinetop. She carefully composed her expression. "I'm sure Doc Anderson will find somebody before too long." She glanced at a nearby end table and noticed that a bowl of onion dip was emptying fast. "Whoops, better get that filled up, Clem," she said brightly. "I wouldn't want people going hungry."

She picked up the bowl and continued toward the kitchen, doing her best to view Clem's news in a philosophical light. It was better that she had found out the truth now, she told herself valiantly, before she got too deeply involved. For the first time she felt not one shred of regret over setting up tonight's party to keep Dan at arm's length. The law of the jungle. Self-preservation. Now, if she could only keep on thinking that way and forget how his kiss had made her feel. . . .

Blunder followed her through the swinging door, eyeing the bowl she carried and wagging his long plumy tail hopefully. Mary Jo was there, getting a Coke from the bucket of ice on the floor next to the kitchen table. When she straightened, her expression was so woebegone that Cassie blurted, "Mary Jo! What's wrong?"

Mary Jo's smile was unconvincing. "Wrong? Nothing's wrong."

"Don't try to kid me, Mary Jo. I know you, remember?"

Mary Jo sighed. "It's Jack. He's been pressuring me for a commitment."

"Marriage?" Cassie crossed to the refrigerator and took out a plastic bowl filled with dip.

"Not quite, but I have the feeling that's the next step." Mary Jo's lips twisted. "I still don't think I'm ready to make any promises, but then he kisses me or sometimes even just *looks* at me and . . ."

"I know exactly what you mean," Cassie muttered. That
was the problem she'd been having with Dan, more and more
each time she saw him. His sensual appeal kept interfering
with her common sense. But no more. Clem's news that Dan
had actually refused to buy Doc Anderson's practice had
surely strengthened her resolve.

Fortunately Mary Jo was too caught up in her own problems to notice Cassie's remark. In a lowered voice, she said,
"And when we make love . . ." Her pupils darkened and her
mouth curved in a dreamy smile.

"That good, huh?" said Cassie dryly. She got a spoon from
a drawer and filled the smaller bowl with dip. "So what are
you going to do about it?"

"I don't know. Right now, I keep trying to avoid the issue,
but the only way I've been able to do that is by avoiding Jack."
Her mouth drooped unhappily. "I've been so mean to him
lately, I just hate myself. But I don't know what else to do."

The door swung open. Dan's dark head poked into the
kitchen. He looked at Cassie, then at Mary Jo. "Oops! Sorry,
ladies. I didn't mean to intrude."

"Why, you weren't intruding, Doc," Mary Jo said gaily.
"Come on in." She glanced at Cassie. "I'll take the dip out."
She took the bowl and walked through the swinging door.
Blunder followed her. Blunder was very fond of onion dip.

"I was just coming to get myself a beer," Dan said.

"I was just getting you one."

"I didn't expect you to wait on me."

"No problem. Just playing hostess," she said. Cassie felt
awkward being alone with Dan—even though there was a
houseful of people only a swinging door away. Don't be so
dumb, she admonished herself. He was hardly going to leap
on her right here in the kitchen with so many Pinetoppers as
a potential audience. And if he did get . . . cozy, she'd put a

stop to it. No more nonsense like the kiss outside the Pizza Bar.

She gestured at the bucket filled with ice and a variety of canned and bottled beer and soft drinks. "Help yourself."

Dan plucked a beer can from amid the ice cubes, then stepped back and lounged against the wall. Cassie went to the refrigerator and took out a fresh six-pack of Coke. As she set the six-pack on the counter to pry the plastic holder loose, the swinging door again opened. Marj Simmons said, "Oh, there you are, Cassie. When are we going to get started? Howdy, Doc. Nice to see you."

"It'll be a few minutes yet," Cassie said. "I want to make sure there are enough supplies before we start."

"Nice to see you, too," Dan murmured, but it was too late. Marj had already retreated. As the door closed, he said, "What was that about? What's going to get started?"

"Charades. And I hope you're ready for it. We have some demon charade players here in Pinetop."

Dan's jaw dropped. "Charades? I didn't know people still played charades."

"Here, we do."

He chuckled. "Talk about turning back the clock."

She had to move closer to him to put the Cokes in the bucket. But she didn't want to go over there . . . as if it might be dangerous to get too close. *Ridiculous!* she thought. Weren't her defenses supposed to be stronger now that she knew what she knew? Odd, but they didn't feel strong. They felt wobbly. Like her knees, which had the strangest inclination, as she deposited the Cokes in the bucket, to carry her the rest of the way across the kitchen, right smack up against Dan Faraday's tall, lean body.

Hoping a touch of discord might cut the attraction pulling her toward him, she said challengingly, "You don't like it very much here, do you?"

"I didn't say that."

"That's how it sounded."

"It may have sounded that way," he said patiently, "but that's not how I feel. It's just different, that's all. If you moved to L.A., it'd take you some time to get used to it, wouldn't it?"

Her mouth twisted. "Forever wouldn't be long enough." City life, city people; it was all one in her book. But even knowing for certain now that Dan was at heart a city type and only a temporary visitor to Pinetop, it was tough not to think of how well and easily he seemed to be fitting in with her friends.

Just one more example of her silly, stupid wishful thinking, she realized with a sigh. She knew she had a tendency to be overly optimistic. Usually she felt that was an okay way to be. Better than gloomily foreseeing problems that never happened. But not now! Not about Dan Faraday. Pollyannas could get badly burnt.

Dan looked at her closely, then made a shrewd guess. "You know L.A., don't you? I mean, more than just as a visitor."

She nodded. "I lived there for nearly five years. Four years in college and then I stayed on to work for a while."

"College?"

Though he tried to master it, Cassie could hear the astonishment in his voice. "Don't sound so surprised," she said. "This may be the mountains, but we aren't hicks up here. Quite a few of the Pinetop kids go to college."

He stepped away from the wall and moved slightly closer to her, his long fingers curled around the frosty beer can. "I'm not surprised. Just . . . curious, I guess. What did you major in?"

"Art."

"Art! No kidding. You paint and draw?" He frowned. "But you don't have a single thing hanging in the living room."

Dan had noticed the blank walls. Though there was nothing elegant about the house, its coziness and comfort created an aesthetic all their own, except for the complete lack of wall decorations.

"Painting, mostly. The year I worked in L.A., I was a very junior sketch artist at a small advertising firm. But now I work mostly in quick-drying acrylics. As far as the walls go, you obviously didn't look closely enough or you'd have seen the picture hangers all over the place."

He frowned. "I don't get it."

"It's simple. I took everything down a couple of weeks ago. I don't get much chance to paint during the tourist season, so, every fall, I take down the stuff I did the previous winter. It kind of encourages me to get going and fill up the walls again."

"What happens to the paintings you take down?"

"I take them over to Alison's place." At Dan's look of incomprehension, she explained, "The dark-haired woman with the silver streak. She was asking me about my stuff just a little while ago, as a matter of fact. She owns the Pinetop Gallery."

"No kidding! I was in there the other day. The pieces on display were really very good." He went on, more slowly, "There was one of a horse in the snow, just kind of suggested, as if he was half snowbank, that I liked a lot. I've been thinking about buying it."

Cassie's eyes sparkled. "If you decide you want it, I'll see if I can talk Alison into giving you a special price."

"You don't need to do that."

"Why not? It's my painting. I should have some say about what it sells for."

Dan gazed at her in open astonishment. "You did that? I had no idea . . . You can really paint, Cassie!"

"Thank you, kind sir." She curtsied. "It's only a hobby, but I enjoy it."

"You don't ever think about painting full-time?"

"Nope. I don't think I'd like it half as much if I *had* to do it. Besides, I really enjoy working with the horses, too."

"I see." He paused. He had planned to tackle this topic later on, but who knew if they'd be alone again this evening? As she tore open a fresh bag of tortilla chips and dumped them on a plate, he said, "Change of subject time. It's my considered opinion that you reneged on our deal."

"Oh?" Cassie tensed. "What deal was that?"

"You know perfectly well what deal."

"I guess you'll have to refresh my memory."

"Okay, I'll spell it out. The deal was that I'd go to the auction with you tomorrow if you went out with me tonight."

"We're out. You're out, anyway, even if I'm at home."

He rolled his eyes. "Looks like we've got a champion hair splitter here. The deal was that we'd spend some time alone."

"We are alone." She continued working. Now, she stood near the sink, her back to Dan as she spooned guacamole into a small bowl from the larger container she'd taken from the fridge. From beyond the swinging door came the continuous thrum of conversation.

"If you call this alone, I guess I can, too." As he spoke, he slipped his arms around her waist from behind and rested his chin on top of her head. "Your hair smells wonderful," he said huskily. His hands moved a little lower on her waist so his fingers splayed across her hip bones. He pulled her more tightly against him.

A hardening bulge beneath the tight confinement of his jeans pressed into Cassie's derriere. Her heart began to pound and her mouth went dry as a wave of desire spread through her.

Unembarrassed, he said, "There! Feel what you do to me?"

The spoon dropped from Cassie's limp fingers into the guacamole. She swallowed hard. "As a matter of fact, I do seem to feel . . . something or other."

The noise of conversation in the next room seemed distant, blotted out by the pulsing of blood in her ears. She covered his hands with her own, uncertain whether she meant to lift them away from her or encourage him to hold her more tightly still.

Now was the moment to remind herself of Dan's temporary status here in Pinetop and in her life. She dutifully did so. But her body didn't seem to care. The feel of him pressed against her was exquisite. Just a moment longer, she thought. A little body contact. What harm could it do? And it felt *so* good.

As if the touch of her hands had been a signal, he bent his head. His breath on her ear made little shivers of delight ripple through her. He took her earlobe between his lips. "Mmm. You taste good, too," he murmured.

The tip of his tongue darted into her ear and Cassie heard a throaty wordless sound come from her own lips.

Dan drew a deep breath. He knew that what he was about to do could be a tactical mistake. She might be outraged. Knowing Cassie, he knew she might retaliate. An elbow in the ribs. Or the heel of her cowboy boot rapped sharply on his shin. But he was at a point where he almost couldn't help himself. His palms ached to know the shape of her. And that little sound of desire she had made encouraged him. His hands slid up her rib cage to cover her breasts.

Cassie was speechless. Her nipples burned at his touch and hardened; they seemed to be trying to poke through her sweater for closer contact with his palms. Her back arched involuntarily and Dan, responding to her wordless cue, rubbed his thumbs back and forth across her tight, aching nipples.

"Good God, Cassie!" he said hoarsely. "Do you have any idea how much I want you?"

She thought she had a pretty good idea. She was heavy and hot; desire gathered in her lower body. It took all her strength to say weakly, "Dan, you have to stop. Someone might come in." She had other reasons, too, why she couldn't let him do this. Unfortunately, at the moment, she couldn't quite get a grasp on what they were.

"You said we were alone," he countered, his hands still moving on her breasts.

"Okay, I lied," she said.

"You admit you reneged on our deal?" His breath was hot on her neck.

The hypnotic rhythm of his thumbs on her throbbing nipples had triggered a longing, a growing need inside her. She'd admit anything, if only he wouldn't stop. But that was wrong. Backward. She *wanted* him to stop. Half the town could burst in at any moment to observe the show. And besides, she remembered now what Clem had told her. So what had happened to her renewed determination not to get involved with Dan? The mere touch of his hands had virtually destroyed it . . . which just went to show how weak *she* was, where he was concerned.

"All right," she said breathlessly. "You win."

"The thing is," he said as if he hadn't heard her, "I know we need to get to know each other better, but how can we do that if you won't spend any time alone with me?"

The rhythm of his hands was stronger, more demanding. Her knees were weakening. She braced her palms on the counter to shore herself up and said, "Dan, stop! I said 'You win!'"

He froze, then stepped away from her. With the loss of contact, she felt perversely both relieved and deprived. Her heart gradually settled back into a more normal rhythm, but her desire would not subside. She turned slowly to face him.

He said cautiously, "You mean . . ."

"We can spend some time alone together," she confirmed. She leaned casually on the counter, hoping Dan wouldn't realize it was because she needed the support. If only it hadn't felt so good for him to hold her. If only her breasts weren't swollen and tender from that brief contact with his hands. If only the clamor of desire in her lower body would settle back to the dull continuous hum of need she had been feeling for days now.

"When?" Dan asked tersely.

Cassie thought furiously. What had she gone and done now? If he could evoke such intense desire in her with a houseful of people a swinging door away, what would happen when they were genuinely alone?

You know what'll happen, she told herself. You'll start ripping his clothes off . . . if he doesn't undress you first.

For a moment, it sounded to her like a terrific idea. Her fingertips itched to touch the buttons closing Dan's shirt, undo them slowly, then slide the garment off his broad shoulders, and feast her eyes on his naked chest.

She put an abrupt halt to *that* train of thought by forcibly reminding herself of her conversation with Clem. Sooner or later, Doc Anderson *would* sell his practice to someone, but not to Dan. And that would mean he would leave.

She looked at Dan. He was watching her, waiting for her answer. She had already promised they could spend some time alone together. She couldn't go back on her word now.

But there was alone and alone, wasn't there? Nothing in their deal said they had to be alone together *indoors*.

"Tomorrow morning," she said decisively. "Before we drive down to Banning for the sale, why don't we go horseback riding?" Nothing could be safer than that, she thought. If it had been summer, even a ride would have had its perils. A bed of pine boughs out in the forest. Horses tethered nearby. Sunlight slanting through the trees to stripe naked bodies with gold.

The mental pictures made her heart skip a beat. Fortunately it was much too cold for hanky-panky in the woods this time of year.

A fleeting scowl crossed Dan's face. "A horseback ride wasn't exactly what I had in mind." A *slight* understatement, he thought sarcastically. "I was thinking more of dinner. A movie." Bringing her home and making passionate love to her. "Something along those lines," he finished.

"Somehow, I kind of figured that." Her tone was wry.

"And?" Dan prompted. One part of him was looking forward with some amusement to hearing what excuses she'd come up with. Another part wished only that she'd cut the evasions and avoidances and admit that the attraction between them was too strong to be denied. But at least he was making some kind of progress, he told himself. Soon, very soon, it would be time to bring the issue into the open, and ask her directly why she was trying to keep their relationship from developing the intimacy they both knew was just plain inevitable.

"Uh, the movie..." she said. "Gee, that sounds like a great idea, Dan. But I'm afraid..."

"Yes?"

"The only thing showing in town right now is an old Disney flick and I've seen it before," she said in a rush.

"I see. And dinner. Why can't we have dinner?"

For a moment, he thought he had her. But then she said, scarcely missing a beat, "I'm on a diet. A very strict one. Yogurt and... and cabbage leaves."

"Funny. You don't look like you need to diet." He paused. "And it's a strange thing. I could have sworn I saw you digging a potato chip into the bean dip a while back."

"Oh no. That couldn't have been me," she said solemnly.

Dan gave a slight shake of his head. "Cassie..." There was a warning note in his voice.

She let out a sigh. "Okay, Dan. No more fooling around. The truth is, I'm just not ready for anything more than a horseback ride." Why had she said 'not ready'? she wondered. That seemed to hold out a promise that eventually...

"So it's take it or leave it?" Dan asked crisply. "The horseback ride or nothing?"

"I'm afraid so."

"Then I'll take it." Her offer wasn't all *that* bad, he decided. He wanted them to get to know each other. Where better than in her element—on horseback? He recognized her ploy for what it was—one more avoidance of the explosion of desire that was bound to happen the moment the circumstances were right. But he could deal with it. Though the need to make love to her was now a constant torment, that wasn't all he wanted. He wanted them to talk to each other, to exchange all the little details of likes and dislikes, to venture a degree of self-revelation.

"I have to admit something, though," he said. "I haven't ridden since I was a kid. And then it was only once or twice."

She regarded him in disbelief. "But you said you've been treating horses for years."

"Racehorses. You don't exactly go out for a trail ride on one of those."

Cassie burst out laughing. "Then I'd say it's about time you found out what a horse is really for."

The swinging door opened. Ellen gazed at Dan accusingly. "So it's you that's holding things up, Doc. Come on, Cassie. You've got people itching for charades out here."

DAN HELD UP THREE FINGERS.

"Third word," said Harry Greville. Harry had evidently left his nephew in charge of the Pizza Bar tonight. Harry's extremely pregnant wife gazed at Harry as if his words revealed sheer genius.

Dan nodded with vigor. He was last man up for the Blue team. They were racing against the clock to beat the Orange team, and it was all up to him. What perverted mind, he wondered, had come up with the song title he was expected to act out? It was impossible.

He tugged his ear.

"Sounds like," Harry said promptly, winning another adoring gaze from his spouse.

Dan mimed stuffing something in his mouth and chewing with great gusto.

Dan was surprised how much fun he was having. It was simple, unsophisticated fun, and he couldn't think when he'd had a better time at a party. Now, if only the members of his team would catch on.

"Food," said one of his team members.

Dan pretended to unwrap something, then devour the contents. He smiled maniacally and rubbed his stomach.

"Good."

"Delicious."

"Eat."

"Rolaids," said one of the jokers in the group.

Dan shook his head and tried again, this time pretending to chew with his mouth full.

"Candy." It was Cassie's voice.

He looked her full in the face and nodded, then tugged his ear to remind her.

"Sounds like candy. Handy. Andy. Sandy. . . Dandy?"

He nodded more vigorously still, feeling like one of those dolls that people put in the back windows of their cars.

"Dandy..." Cassie paused, then cried, "'Yankee Doodle Dandy?'"

Dan grinned broadly. "That's it!"

Ellen, the official timekeeper, pondered her watch, then said, "Blue team wins."

Assorted cheers and groans greeted the announcement. The seated players rose and a general post-game milling took place. Dan's back was thumped and he even did some thumping himself as members of the Blue team indulged in a bout of self-congratulation. "Cassie's the one who got it. She deserves the credit," he said more than once. He looked around in search of her and spotted her across the room, talking to Marj and Alison, the art gallery woman.

He started edging toward her. His route took him past Jack and Mary Jo, who had retreated into a private corner. They still seemed to be having problems, he noticed. Her face was white, Jack's red. Though Dan didn't mean to eavesdrop, he couldn't help overhearing Mary Jo say, "You take too much for granted, Jack Webley."

"Aw, c'mon, Mary Jo." The cowboy shuffled his feet. "All I did was ask you—"

"I know what you asked, but I told you. I'm going to stay and help Cassie clean up. And I'm spending the night here, too."

Jack looked astonished. "You didn't say anything about—"

Dan moved past the pair. He had a hunch that Mary Jo's plan to sleep over might be news to Cassie. And he was conscious of his own disappointment. He hadn't expected to batter down Cassie's remaining defenses tonight. In the kitchen, earlier, she'd said she wasn't ready. Well, he could deal with that. He wouldn't *actually* go out of his mind from wanting her. But even so, he'd hoped for a little more time alone with her before the evening ended. A few kisses. An embrace. And a cold shower and another restless night, he thought ironically.

He made it to Cassie's side. "Good job, Champ," he said.

"That's what I should be saying to you." Her face wore an open, happy smile. "'Yankee Doodle Dandy.' That was a tough one."

He put on an exaggeratedly ferocious scowl. "I'd like to get my hands on the person who came up with it."

Marj's smug smile left little doubt who the culprit was.

"Anyhow, you did a great job," Cassie said to him.

"It was fun." He let a teasing note come into his voice. "Really nice party, Cassie."

They shared the joke with a swift meeting of their eyes. Then Marj said, "Well, it's getting late. Anybody seen Joe?" She went off to find her silent husband.

Dan smiled at Alison, the art gallery woman. Next week, he decided impulsively, he'd go in and buy Cassie's painting. He liked it. Liked it a lot. And it would complement the decor in his office. He especially liked the idea of owning something Cassie had created.

He looked down at her and felt a surge of longing. *Down, boy!* he told himself. If he didn't cool it, Alison and anyone else who happened to be watching would see what a state he was in.

Mary Jo stopped a few feet away. "Cassie," she said plaintively, "can I talk to you for a minute?"

"Sure." She stepped aside to join the blonde.

Dan watched as Jack, looking as if his nose was decidedly out of joint, said good-night and left.

The party, having begun to break up, thinned out fast. Cassie became occupied, bidding her guests farewell. After a while, Dan began unobtrusively gathering up plates and glassware. He took a load to the kitchen where he found Mary Jo standing at the sink. Her mouth was set in an unhappy line, but she tried to smile when she saw Dan. "You don't have to do that," she said with a glance at the party debris he set on the counter. "I'm sticking around to help Cassie clean up." She looked more closely at him. "And you wish I weren't, don't you, Doc?"

He restrained a sigh. "No comment."

"I'm sorry."

"Don't worry about it. It's not your fault."

She got an interested gleam in her eye. "Tell you what. I can't vanish or anything, but I do promise to be very busy here in the kitchen for a while." She jerked her head in the direction of the door. "Just about everybody's gone. Play your cards right and . . ."

"Thanks, Mary Jo," he said hastily and headed for the living room.

Cassie was just closing the door on the last of the departing guests. She heard Dan's footsteps and turned to face him. "Dan! Are you still here? I thought you'd gone."

What a liar she was! She had known exactly where he was every second of the evening. It was as if she had a complex radar installation in her brain, whose sole purpose was the tracking of one Dan Faraday. She had known when he laughed, when he crossed his arms, when he sipped his beer.

"Did you really think I'd go without saying good-night?" he asked. "That would be very rude." He stepped forward and slid his arms around her waist as if it was the most natural thing in the world to do.

"No, I didn't really think you would," Cassie admitted. It seemed so unfriendly to just stand there without touching him. Her hands lifted and came to rest on his muscular biceps. But she was *supposed* to be unfriendly, wasn't she? asked a little voice in her mind. But right now it seemed like too much effort.

"Did I apologize for the little joke I played on you tonight, Dan?"

"You mean the party? No, but there's no need. I had a great time. And I expect to have a great time tomorrow on our ride. What time?"

"Is eight too early for you?"

"No, that's fine." He paused. "I'd better get going," he said, but instead of releasing her, he pulled her closer and bent his head.

At the last moment, before his mouth met hers, Cassie murmured "Mary Jo's in the kitchen. She might come out any minute."

"Somehow, I don't think so," Dan said. And then he kissed her long and thoroughly, his tongue intimately invading her mouth. His hands slid down her body, molding her hips to his.

They stood fused together, mouths joined. And Cassie, who knew she shouldn't be letting him do this, who had set up the whole party to keep this from happening, who'd had a strong reminder this very evening of Dan's temporary status, forgot everything except the flicker of his tongue and the hard press of his body.

It had to end or they would adjourn to the bedroom, regardless of Mary Jo. Regardless of anything and everything. Cassie knew it. Dan knew it. He loosened his embrace and just stood there looking at her for a long moment. Then he said good-night.

A few minutes later, Cassie forced her legs to carry her into the kitchen. She had gotten her breathing under control before daring to face Mary Jo, but she feared that the flush of desire was still visible on her face and throat. The ache of unsatisfied passion sat heavily in her lower body and her nipples felt hard and puckered from their contact with Dan's chest.

Hopeful that Mary Jo, who was drying glassware, wouldn't notice these signs, she said, "Okay. Tell me all. What's the current status with you and Jack?"

Mary Jo looked around and started. "Good grief, Cassie! You look like... I don't know what you look like. As if you're in a trance or something."

Cassie sighed. "Maybe I am." She had to be. If she had all her wits about her, she would be concentrating on the reality that Dan Faraday's presence in Pinetop was only temporary. She wouldn't be thinking that it was impossible to postpone the inevitable much longer. Nor would she be regretting Mary Jo's decision to spend the night—which was about all that had kept her from taking Dan by the hand, leading him into her bedroom, and shutting the door.

7

THE SLOPE WAS DENSE with pines and alders; the sun poked narrow fingers through the trees. To the twitter of birds and the rustling of small creatures in the forest was added the music of bits jingling, leather creaking and the regular plod of horses' hooves.

Dan inhaled the crisp piney air. Cassie was right, he thought. This was what a horse was really for.

One of the things, he mentally amended. Watching a gallant Thoroughbred race for the finish line was a different experience, but also powerful.

So far, at least, he hadn't made a fool of himself on horseback. King, the big bay Cassie had given him, was gentle and willing. He wondered why he had never thought of going riding in L.A. Rental stables abounded near Griffith Park— the great chunk of hilly land carved out of the city for public use. It wouldn't have been the same, though. Not like here, where open country went on for mile after mile and they could, if they chose, ride all the way to Rainbow Peak without encountering a car or even a strip of pavement.

He looked at Cassie's back and Kettle's rump, ahead of him on the trail, and wished they could ride abreast so he could share his thoughts with her.

Cassie, leading the way on Kettle, was immersed in thoughts of her own. And just as glad, for the moment, that the trail was so narrow that riding next to Dan was impossible.

The night before, she and Mary Jo had sat up drinking co-coa and talking, like two teenagers rehashing the prom. Mary Jo was distressed that her indecision was making her treat Jack badly. Cassie had no easy answer for her friend. A few weeks before she would have probably said, "Make up your mind. That's all there is to it."

Now, she knew all too well that sometimes a relationship between a man and a woman couldn't be regulated so sim-ply. The case of her and Dan was a good example. Her mind was telling her one thing, her heart and body urging the op-posite course.

She heard a rustle and a flurry in the trees and looked off to one side of the trail to see Blunder bounding away, his plumy tail waving. He was probably after a rabbit. Fortu-nately he never caught anything. He was bred for herding, not for hunting.

For a moment she thought of herself as the fleeing rabbit, Dan the pursuing hound. But she knew the analogy was all wrong. All she, as rabbit, would have to do was stand her ground, say—and mean it—that she didn't want to get in-volved and he would back off. Unfortunately this particular rabbit kept encouraging its pursuer. The way she'd kissed him the night before, her earlier response to the touch of his hands on her body...

But what lay ahead? A passionate love affair? His leav-ing? Heartbreak and loneliness?

The trail widened and Cassie held Kettle back to let Dan catch up with her. "How do you like it so far?" she asked.

"It's great." He was enjoying it all—the scents, the sounds, the shadowed mystery of the forest around them and the steady motion of the horse beneath him. He felt relaxed and at the same time fully alive, all his receptors open to sensa-tion.

Including the sensation of looking at Cassie and wanting her with a ferocity that half scared him. He could so easily imagine the slim legs that now gripped Kettle's sides locked around him in the fervor of an intimate embrace.

"Dan, can I ask you something?"

"Sure. Ask away," he said lightly.

"How come you left that stable? What was it called?"

"Willow Run." His jaw tightened; the reminder seemed to leach the scent from the air and turn the music of birds and jingling bits into simple noise again. "That wasn't the only stable I worked for, though. Just the major one." He knew his voice sounded unnatural as he spoke of it. Again and again he had asked himself why he couldn't let it go, just stop thinking about it and get on with his life. And he had figured out that what had happened represented the first real failure of his adult life. It galled him. But he would show them. He'd come back somehow, achieve an even better position in the racing world than he'd had before. Those who had believed the stories about him would have to eat them.

Cassie saw the expression in his eyes and tensed, disturbing Kettle who jogged nervously beneath her. "Easy, fella," she said, patting the shining neck. Anger and pain had mingled in Dan's eyes, along with a momentary blaze of determination. And he still hadn't answered her question. "I'm sorry. I didn't mean to pry."

"You weren't prying. It's just . . ." He wouldn't let this reminder spoil the morning. To discuss it now would be to poison the idyll. He said apologetically, "It's something I'd rather not talk about right now, if you don't mind."

"Oh, sure," she said quickly. "I understand. There are things I don't like to talk about, too."

He threw her a curious glance. "Like what?"

She sighed. "Right now, I can't think of a single thing." She turned in the saddle and made a sweeping gesture. "Look!"

They had reached the margin of the trees. The horses emerged from the timberline onto a stony ridge. On either side the mountain sloped away, giving a compass view of the land below. Pinetop's buildings, nestled in a shallow valley, were tiny blocks thrown down by a giant's hand.

Behind the town Rainbow Peak rose, an imposing craggy fist thrust against the sky. The pale winter sun painted the granite with shades of pink and gold. Far, far below, the flat desert floor was shrouded by distance into a muted blur of browns and tans.

Dan sucked in his breath in appreciation. "It's beautiful." He stood up in his stirrups, not only to see a little farther, but to ease the stiffness he had accumulated during the hour-long ride.

Cassie noticed and said sympathetically, "I'm afraid you're going to be sore tomorrow."

"No, I'll be fine. I wouldn't mind dismounting for a minute, though."

They had reached a level patch of rocky ground. Cassie reined Kettle in and swung lightly to the ground, then lifted the reins over the horse's head and let the knotted ends dangle on the stony earth.

More laboriously, Dan dismounted. He was about to let go of King's reins as he had seen Cassie do with Kettle's when she said, "You'd better not drop his reins, Dan. Kettle's ground-tied—trained not to move when his reins are dragging—but King isn't."

"Then what am I supposed to do with him?" There wasn't a thing around to tie the animal to. Not a tree or shrub; not even a jutting rock.

Cassie chuckled. "I guess you'll just have to hang on to him. Unless you feel like walking back."

"Okay." He grasped the end of the reins in one hand. "It's going to be damned inconvenient, but I guess I'll manage."

"Manage what?" Cassie asked, then, slightly embarrassed, guessed he might need to go down the slope into the scrub to relieve himself. She held out her hand. "It's okay. I'll hold his reins for you."

"Will you? That's nice. Thanks." He extended his hand for her to take King's reins, then just kept on coming until both his arms were around her waist. He looked down at her and said, "Thanks for the morning, Cassie. It's wonderful."

"I'm glad you're enjoying it." His arms were only lightly looped around her. A single step would have set her free. But she couldn't seem to move away from him. He bent his head, and it felt so right for her to tilt her face up to welcome his kiss.

But just before his mouth met hers, Dan hesitated. King's long equine nose was at Dan's shoulder, and he was nuzzling Dan's ear. Gently but firmly, he pushed the horse's head away. "Not exactly what I had in mind, old fellow."

Cassie took the opportunity to step away from Dan, King's reins looped over her arm. "Saved by the bell. Thanks, King," she said, trying to make a joke of it.

A frown flickered across Dan's face. "Saved... That's a funny thing to say."

"I'm sorry. I didn't mean it as an insult. It's just..." Her voice trailed away.

"Just what?" he prompted. When she didn't answer, he said, "Now, Cassie, listen. I think it's time we talked about what's going on between us."

"I think we should, too."

He said gravely, "You see, I get conflicting messages from you. Until today, you've gone to great lengths to avoid being alone with me and yet, when I kiss you..."

He didn't have to elaborate. She knew exactly what he meant. She looked down at the design on the toes of her boots. "I know. I . . . I like you, Dan and, I have to admit it, I'm strongly attracted to you, but . . ."

"I knew there was a but."

She drew a deep breath. With the feeling that this was a last-ditch effort, and about as futile as shaking a finger to stave off a whirlwind, she said, "But I keep telling myself that I shouldn't get involved with you."

He sounded surprised. "Is there a reason?"

"Uh-huh. A good one."

"Really? Something reprehensible about my character that I'm not aware of?" His smile was strained. "I don't torture small animals, Cassie. Really I don't, although I have to admit that some of my patients seem to think that's what I have in mind."

She smiled back at him, but, like Dan's, her smile quickly faded. "It's nothing like that. The problem is, you're leaving Pinetop. You're only here for a while. You've made no bones about that." She tried to keep it light, but she could hear the unhappiness in her voice. "Why, for all I know, you could take off tomorrow."

So *that* was it, Dan thought. He should have guessed, should have realized. But it wasn't as if he were in Pinetop for only a few days or even a few weeks. Doc Anderson had said that it would probably take several months before he found the right person to sell his practice to. There was *time*. Time for his relationship with Cassie to develop. Time for them to find out what they were going to mean to each other.

"It won't be that soon," he said.

She shrugged. "So, big deal. We're talking about weeks instead of days. Don't you see, Dan? There's no point to it."

His dark gaze seemed to burrow into her. "Don't *you* see, Cassie? Just because it won't necessarily last forever doesn't mean it can't be good. For both of us. And besides . . . things happen."

Yeah, like her falling hopelessly in love with Dan Faraday and getting her heart broken, Cassie thought. "What kind of . . . things are you talking about?"

"Who knows? I might end up staying longer than I think. Or . . ." His voice trailed away.

Hope flooded her. She wanted to hear him say that there was at least a possibility that he might stay not just "longer," but decide that this was the place where he wanted to spend the rest of his life. Her voice was slightly tremulous. "Or what?"

"It's premature, I know, to even mention it, but our relationship *could* develop to the point that you could decide to come with me when I go."

Her heart plummeted to the rocky ground and lay there. "Oh," she said in a thin, small voice.

He looked at her acutely. "Oh?"

"I know we're just talking theoretically, Dan, but I couldn't do that. I'd never leave Pinetop."

He had pulled his gloves off, she noticed. Now he ran the fingers of one hand through his hair in a gesture of frustration. "So you won't get involved with me because I'm not planning to stay here forever. And yet, from what I've heard, none of the permanent residents light your fires. Not the way it is with us."

"That's true," she admitted.

"Has it occurred to you that you've set up some pretty tough rules for yourself, lady?"

"What do you mean?"

"I mean, you've put yourself in a real bind, haven't you? What are you going to do, Cassie? Wait until some guy shows up in town and swears on a stack of Bibles that he's never, *ever* going to leave Pinetop, no matter what happens, and *then* maybe you'll consider developing a relationship with him? Pinetop's a small town. There's not a lot of turnover in the population. It could be years before that happens."

He was making her determination sound silly. And she had to admit that he had a point. Several points. She hadn't really minded her years of celibacy, but that was before Dan Faraday had come along to remind her of what it felt like to give and receive love. "I know that," she said.

"I'm sure you do. You're an intelligent woman . . . except when it comes to this one thing. You've got these rules, and they've got you blocked in, like a horse in a too-small stall. You haven't left yourself any way to turn."

The image seemed to illuminate her problem in a new way. What *was* she supposed to do? Go on and on alone until the very capacity for passion was leached out of her by time? She looked at him, then said hesitantly, "In a way, I guess you're right. I'll think about what you've said, Dan. Okay?"

"Okay. That's all I'm asking . . . at the moment." He paused. "No, I'm asking one thing more. I understand your point of view on this—even if I don't think it makes a whole lot of sense. Now, I want you to hear mine."

"That's fair."

He closed the gap between them. He did not put his arms around her, but with his chest only inches away, his dark eyes fixed on her face, she felt as if they were in an embrace. In a low husky voice, he said, "I want you, Cassie, more than I've ever wanted a woman in my entire life. It's all I can think about lately. When I'm with you. When I'm with other people. When I'm alone. It's all the same. All I can think about is you."

His words had started her heart pounding. *It's the same for me,* she wanted to tell him. He was in her thoughts, in her heart, night and day. Not yet, she cautioned herself. She had to think about what he'd said. She had to decide if she should break her promise to herself that she wouldn't get involved with any man, unless there was at least the *possibility* of forever.

He lifted one hand and traced the curve of her cheek. "One more thing for you to think about," he said and his mouth greedily took hers.

It was a different kind of kiss from the others he'd given her, possessive and plundering, as if he meant to demonstrate the force of his need. His tongue plunged rhythmically into her mouth, presaging the sexual act. Cassie's body recognized the demonstration and responded. Her hips moved against his, desire gathering turgidly within her, as if they were unclothed together. His erection seemed to burn through their two sets of clothing; she could feel its outline imprinting her flesh.

Dan groaned, then, still kissing her, made enough space between them to reach for the tab at the throat of her jacket. He pulled the zipper down swiftly and spread the sides of her jacket apart. Beneath, she wore a sweatshirt. Unglamorous attire, but practical for a ride. No bra; she hadn't thought she'd needed one. And now she realized that it made no difference at all. At this moment, chain mail couldn't have kept Dan from touching her. He slid his hand beneath her sweatshirt, then caressed upward until her breast was in his palm. Cassie gave a little moan of pleasure, and her head dropped back as he took her nipple between thumb and forefinger.

He lifted his mouth from hers. With both hands, he spread her jacket wider, then pushed her sweatshirt up so her breasts were bared. The cold air was a shock. Almost unpleasant. But before she started shivering, Dan covered one of her breasts with his hand. He bent his head toward the other. His tongue laved her nipple, creating a pleasure so intense that she felt as if she were melting, drowning in it. When he surrounded the tight bud with his mouth, tugging gently, she let out a breathless cry.

Eyes closed, abandoned to the sensations flooding her body, Cassie reached out and put her hand on the front of his jeans. Urgently she needed to know with her palm what she had felt with her belly. He was hard and hot, and when she touched him, that most masculine part of him leaped against her hand.

She rubbed her hand over him for a moment, then touched the snap at the waistband of his jeans, wanting to feel him naked and freed to her touch. Common sense intervened. They'd end up making love on the rocky ground. And probably die of hypothermia in the process.

Dan seemed to come to his senses at virtually the same moment as she. He lifted his head from her breast, lowered her sweatshirt and drew the fronts of her jacket back together. Then, with a comical grimace that only endeared him to her more, he put his hand on his crotch, seeking to ease the discomfort she knew he must be feeling by shifting the weight beneath. "Damn jeans. I never realized how tight they were before," he grumbled. His arm dropped to his side, and he gazed at her. "We seem to have gotten a bit carried away."

Cassie tried to keep it light, but it was difficult since her breathing was heavy and erratic. "Well, you've given me something to think about all right," she said. Her gaze slid to one side of Dan, and she said sharply, "Damn!"

"What is it?" Dan asked, alarmed.

"It's King. I must have let go of his reins."

The big bay was ambling slowly back in the direction they'd come. As Cassie dashed after the animal, Dan threw back his head and laughed. If he'd needed proof of his effect on her, he'd gotten it . . . in spades.

8

CASSIE DISMOUNTED near the corral fence and waved to Jennifer Pettigrew. The freckle-faced redheaded teenager was working her little chestnut gelding in the arena. Now Jennifer reined her horse near the fence and called, "The rental party got off just fine. They're supposed to be back by ten." She smiled at Dan. "Hi, Doc. Have a nice ride?"

"Very nice," Dan said. He knew Jennifer. The week before, she had brought her dog in for a rabies shot.

He unsaddled King while Cassie gave the girl instructions about feeding the horses that evening. She had mentioned that Jennifer took charge of the stable sometimes, in return for a reduced rate on her horse's board.

"I'll meet you here at eleven, then," he confirmed with Cassie, then walked—a little stiff-legged, but trying not to show it—to his van to go back to Doc Anderson's place for a shower and a change of clothes.

As he drove out of the stable yard, Jennifer smiled and said ingenuously, "Doc Faraday's really nice, isn't he?"

"Yes, he is." Cassie tried to keep any betraying inflection out of her voice, but she knew that whether the news that she had been out riding alone with Dan reached the citizens of Pinetop by this afternoon or not until the following day depended solely on when Jennifer next saw her mother. Alice Pettigrew was not exactly a gossip, but she was definitely *interested* in people and their doings. And it looked as if Jennifer was taking after her parent . . .

"AND NOW, FOLKS, lot thirty-two. A gelding. I'm told he's trail savvy and an easy ride for anybody. Starting the bid at two hundred." The auctioneer flowed into his patter. "Two, gimme two, gimme two . . ."

Art's A-1 Weekly Auction had been in full swing for over an hour. Cassie sat on a wooden bench seat. Her eyes were trained on the horse being ridden back and forth inside the wire-enclosed area at the front of the big, barnlike auction room, but her awareness was centered on Dan, seated beside her.

The drive down the mountain in Cassie's pickup truck with her horse trailer attached had been . . . nice, although the word seemed too mild to describe their conversation, often punctuated by laughter. Dan had confessed his ignominious defeat at Tiger's paws, which had led to an exchange of tales about difficult animals each of them had known.

As they neared the desert floor and the temperature rose, the conversation had moved to a more personal level. Childhoods. Parents. They had covered the basics by the time Cassie parked in the lot next to the auction barn.

In the back of her mind the whole way, however, had been thoughts of their talk up on the mountain. With every mile of curving descent, she had become more and more convinced that Dan was right. *No one* going into a love affair received any advance guarantees that it would last forever. With her insistence on not getting involved with anyone who wasn't a permanent Pinetopper, she might be giving up her chances for life and joy.

"Sold!" shouted the auctioneer, and horse and rider exited.

Lot thirty-three came in, ridden by a young man wearing jeans, a T-shirt and a navy blue billed cap. The horse was a flashy pinto, white with great splashes of black on its rump, shoulders and neck.

Cassie pulled her buyer's number from her purse. The pinto was the only horse she planned to bid on today. Dan had checked both the Bob Manners-trained horses being offered for sale, but he had nixed the other, a pretty chestnut mare. He suspected, he had told Cassie, that the animal had a partially detached retina, with consequent loss of sight in one eye. Cassie had immediately given up any thought of bidding on the mare. A partly blind horse could be dangerous at dusk or in shadows, inclined to lose its footing or to spook at objects that suddenly appeared on its blind side.

As the young rider showed off the pinto's paces, moving back and forth in the narrow, sawdust-covered aisle behind the wire fencing, the auctioneer called, "Start at three. Three, gimme three, gimme..." A hand went up. The auctioneer, a red-faced, heavyset man, continued without pause, "Three twenty-forty, twenty-forty..."

The auctioneer's continuous flow asked for twenty-dollar jumps. A hand holding a buyer's number shot up in the air. Almost at once, another hand, off to the side, was lifted. Evidently, Cassie wasn't the only person there who knew that the skilled Bob Manners had trained the pinto.

When the bidding reached five hundred, Cassie raised her buyer's number, hoping that this was a point when others would decide to drop out. For a moment, she thought she had it. But then, a rapid-fire succession of bids pushed the price upward. She bid once more, at six-forty, but when the numbers passed seven hundred, she shrugged and said quietly, "Too much for me."

Dan glanced at her face. Since she wanted this horse, he wanted her to have it. He was even tempted to keep bidding, buy the horse, and give it to her. *Bad idea, Dan*, he told himself. She might think—though she would be wrong—that he was trying to use money to influence the course of their relationship.

If there even was a relationship... He hoped there was. He hoped he had shaken her resolve not to get involved with anyone who wasn't a permanent resident of Pinetop, but he couldn't be sure what she would decide. It *was* a silly rule she had made for herself, he thought. It wasn't as if he was suggesting a one-night stand...

"Sold!" The auctioneer pointed to a man in a cowboy hat seated off to one side. "Eight-twenty."

Dan looked at Cassie. "I hope you aren't too disappointed."

She shrugged lightly. "It's no big deal. I would have liked to have had the pinto. The customers love that flashy look. But in a way, it's better I didn't get him. Now he won't be eating his head off all winter and not doing any work. I'll wait till spring to buy another horse." She smiled. "I'm just sorry I dragged you down here for nothing."

"It wasn't for nothing. I've had a great time." Mostly because he was with Cassie, he thought. He had discovered she was well-known and well liked by the local horse crowd. As they walked up and down the rows of pipe corrals where the horses were kept until their turn to be auctioned off, it had seemed as if no more than a few seconds elapsed without someone greeting her, stopping to talk, being introduced by her to Dan.

He had been unable to keep from comparing this sale to the Thoroughbred auctions he had attended in the past. At those auctions, both people and horses reeked of money in great quantities—expensive clothes, gleaming highly polished equine hides. Here everyone, both human and horse, was a little shaggier, a little shabbier. And yet, when people and horses got together, especially at a sale, the air of suppressed excitement was always the same, whether you were talking about a million-dollar colt at the Lexington Yearling Sales or a tough trail-wise mare at Art's A-1 Weekly Auction.

"I'm ready to go if you are," Cassie said.

"Sure." As he rose, he glanced at his watch. It was a little past four. He'd hoped the sale might go late enough that he could suggest they have dinner before driving back up the mountain. With Jennifer looking after the stable, they didn't actually *have* to hurry. But he could hardly claim starvation at this hour.

So he'd ask her later, he decided. No reason they couldn't eat in Pinetop. The Pine Tree Inn was supposed to be excellent.

He wondered what she'd say. Had their conversation this morning gotten to her at all? Or would the mention of dinner—awfully like an actual date—send her running for cover?

His jaw tensed, lips firming. He had never felt Neanderthal about a woman before, never felt a longing for the good old days when a man could bonk his chosen mate over the head and drag her off to his cave. Now he could see definite advantages to the system. Except that, as much as he wanted Cassie, he wanted her willing . . . as eager to share his bed as he was to make endless passionate love to her.

They had edged down the row of seats, excusing themselves when forced to climb over people's legs. As they reached the aisle, a horse was led, not ridden, into the display area at the front of the room. Dan saw it from the corner of his eye, then turned his head for a closer look and sucked in his breath, feeling as if he'd been socked in the stomach. Nothing that looked like *that* had ever gone on sale at an auction he'd attended before.

The horse was pathetically thin. Its sides were hollowed, knobby hipbones sticking up beneath a rough, dull brown coat. It was a mare, Dan saw. Her head hung low, looking too heavy for the emaciated neck, and she walked shakily, as if each step might be her last.

"Let's go," he said to Cassie, forcing a cheerful expression onto his face. He hoped to get her out of there before she noticed the pitiful creature who was now just standing in front of the auctioneer's podium.

But she had already seen. Her eyes were wide and hurt looking as she gazed at the horse. There was a brief pause; one of the auctioneer's assistants showed the red-faced man something on a clipboard. The mare stared hopelessly at the sawdust.

Without looking at Dan, Cassie grabbed his wrist and tugged him down beside her into a pair of vacant seats on the aisle. "Sorry," she said. "I can't go quite yet. There's something I have to do first."

Dan looked at her, mildly perplexed. "What?"

"I came to buy a horse," she said. "And I'm going to buy one." She pointed toward the brown mare. "That one."

"Cassie, you can't!"

"Oh yes, I can." Her face was determined. "Just watch me."

"But the poor thing's on her last legs. She might die any minute."

"She might," Cassie said. "But then again, she might not. Banjo didn't and she looked almost as bad as that mare when I bought her. And then there's Eagle and Lady." She never took her eyes off the horse. "You haven't met them—I keep them pastured year round—but they're doing just fine." A shadow of remembered pain crossed her face. "I did lose Ginger and Dandy, but at least they had a chance."

Dan stared at her. "You've bought all those horses . . ."

"And they all looked almost as bad as Princess," she confirmed.

"Princess?"

She nodded her head toward the mare. "That's what I'm going to call her after I buy her."

Light dawned gradually on Dan as he put together things she'd said. "That's why you never get money ahead to paint and fix up the stable," he guessed. "Your profits go to take care of derelict horses. How many have you bought so far?"

"Not *that* many, Dan. Eight, I guess. Or nine." She looked at him, slightly defiant, as if she expected his disapproval.

He said softly, "It's not a very practical thing to do, I guess, but—" impulsively, he put his arm around her shoulders and hugged her "—I think it's terrific! In fact, I'll be glad to help. If you need any extra money . . ."

"Thanks, Dan." The smile she gave him made him feel warm all over. "But the money's no problem. I'll be able to get Princess for ninety . . . a hundred dollars, tops."

"How can you be so sure of the price?"

"Any higher than that and the other bidders won't take a chance on her."

Dan frowned. "There are other people who do the same thing you do?"

"Not quite. There are a couple of guys here—" her gaze went to a heavyset man in a brightly flowered Hawaiian shirt, a white cowboy hat perched above a round face "—who buy horses like Princess and gamble they can fatten them up a little." Her lips thinned; her voice was tight. "Horsemeat's quite a delicacy in France, you know."

"I see," he said slowly. A hundred dollars wasn't a lot of money, he thought, but it was only the beginning of her expenses when she rescued a failing or abused animal. Feed. Medicine. Shoeing. Veterinary care. At least he could help her there. As long as he was in Pinetop, he vowed, Cassie would never receive another vet bill.

She was on target with the price, Dan soon discovered. Whatever problem had been occupying the auctioneer and his assistant was resolved. The bidding on Princess, as Dan already thought of the mare, began at, "Thirty, gimme

thirty," and in less than two minutes, Cassie was the mare's
new owner, for ninety dollars.

Ten minutes after that, Princess was tied to the back of
Cassie's trailer. Dan ran his hands gently over the dull coat.
"No obvious signs of disease," he reported after a quick pre-
liminary examination. "Though I'll have to do blood tests and
X rays to be certain. And, of course, she's no spring
chicken . . ."

He went to the mare's head and lifted her upper lip. She
seemed too ill or defeated to object when he pried her mouth
open to examine her teeth. "Good girl," he said, patting the
mare. He let her close her mouth, then turned to Cassie. "I
can't tell for sure without tests, but I think I just found the
basic problem. No one's had her teeth rasped in years. They're
not lining up."

"She can't chew. Maybe hasn't been able to chew for a long
time," Cassie said sadly.

Dan nodded. "She's been starving. In a field full of grass,
she would have starved. There's a little more to it, of course.
She's at an age when she might need some softer food anyway—mashes and so forth. And there may be other problems I haven't found yet, but with some soft food and her
teeth properly rasped, I'd say she has a chance."

Cassie's smile was so wide, she looked as if her face might
crack. "Come on. Let's load her and get her home."

THE AROMA of steaming bran filled the barn. "I wish it'd cool
faster so I could give it to her," Cassie complained.

Princess was blanketed and in her new stall. Dan had ridden all the way up the mountain in the swaying horse trailer.
He had suggested he could keep an eye on Princess that way
and Cassie, though she was sorry not to have his company,
was relieved that he would be with the aged mare.

While she cooked the mash now steaming in a bucket on the barn floor, he had done a preliminary rasping job on Princess's teeth. The mare had endured it without complaint, which Dan thought a bad sign. Many horses—healthy horses—required sedation before this particular job could be done.

"If she eats, it'll definitely be a hopeful sign," he said.

"And if she doesn't?"

"We'll cross that bridge when we come to it." If necessary, he'd rig up some kind of intravenous feed.

Cassie tested the mash for at least the twentieth time. "I think it's cool enough now," she announced, then hoisted the bucket over the stall door and hung it from a hook.

Princess just stood there, head hanging low. She showed no interest in the aroma wafting from the bucket.

Cassie gave Dan a despairing look. "Oh, Lord! Maybe she's too far gone."

"Don't give up yet," he said. He opened the stall door, scooped up a portion of mash in his bare hand and held it under Princess's nose. "There you are, girl. Just try some of this."

For an endless moment, nothing happened. Princess didn't even quiver. But then, her lips opened and mumbled on the mash in Dan's hand. Cassie held her breath and went on holding it until Dan turned. With a broad smile, he showed her his bran-smeared hand. "She took some. Not much, but it's a start."

He scooped out another handful, but this time held it a few inches in front of Princess's nose. "Come and get it, girl. That's it, mama."

Slowly, ever so slowly, Princess stretched her neck forward. Again Dan felt the touch of the soft lips and his hand was emptied. He repeated the process. This time, Princess actually took a step in order to reach the tempting mash.

Then Dan held his mash-filled hand just above the level of the bucket. Princess ate it, then lowered her nose into the bucket.

Dan came out of the stall, grinning broadly. "I think we did it!"

"*You* did it!" Cassie cried. "This is wonderful! You've been so terrific!" Spontaneously, she threw her arms around him. All her thoughts had been on Princess. She was unprepared for the sensual shock the feel of his hard body gave her. And yet part of her had known exactly what would happen at the touch of his hips, his strong thighs. Her breasts flattened against his broad chest. The frosty air in the barn was suddenly so thick that it was difficult for her to breathe.

Dan gave her a one-arm hug, holding his bran-smeared hand away from her. The unexpected body contact made him inhale sharply. Throughout the day his desire for her had only increased. Seeing more of the kind of person she was—the way she was with people, then her altruistic efforts on behalf of an otherwise doomed horse—had made him realize that his body was pretty smart. Somehow it had known at once what it had taken his mind more time to discover—that Cassie McLean was an extraordinary lady.

He let her go before he was tempted to let the hug become a more intimate embrace, a kiss... He had asked her to think about what he'd said, and he'd promised himself, after that one sizzling kiss, to give her at least a little time to do her thinking.

He said lightly, "People have to eat, too. I was going to invite you to dinner at the Pine Tree tonight..."

She frowned regretfully. "That would have been nice, but..."

"I said I was *going* to invite you, but I figure you won't want to go very far from Princess."

She nodded. "I want to be able to check on her, at least every hour or so."

"That's what I thought." He bowed with a flourish. "So the Pine Tree's going to come to us."

Cassie chuckled. "I don't think they have a take-out window."

"Even so, I'm sure it can be arranged." Even if it meant cash passing into the appropriate hands, he thought.

THE MASH BUCKET was empty and Princess dozed in her stall. Dan had left Cassie watching the mare while he went to the Pine Tree. Satisfied that they'd done all that could be done for Princess at the moment, Cassie left the barn and crossed the yard to the house. On the surface of her mind was her pleasure that Princess had eaten so well, but underneath currents were running deep and strong. Currents that could lead to only one conclusion. She and Dan were going to make love. Tonight.

He had been so helpful with Princess, and she liked the way that help had been freely and enthusiastically given. Yet it only made him harder to resist. She had thought that by avoiding making love with him, she could avoid *falling* in love. A piece of faulty reasoning, she saw now. She was pretty close to loving him already, and there wasn't much she could do to keep from falling the rest of the way unless she ruthlessly cut him out of her life. Refused to see him, at all, anywhere. And that was impossible. Even if the size of Pine-top hadn't made encounters inevitable, she couldn't just shut him out of her life.

What he had said out on the mountain about the bind she was in with her self-imposed rules was all true. But his words also had given her the excuse she'd unconsciously been looking for to give in to her body's and her heart's desires.

She opened the back door of her house, Blunder following at her heels. An un-Cassielike thought came to her—to dress for the occasion. What better way to let Dan know she was ready to make love to him? She could greet him at the door in a slinky teddy. The only problem was, she didn't own a slinky teddy, and she had the feeling that the long flannel underwear she wore in winter wouldn't have quite the right effect.

HOLDING TWO STYROFOAM meal containers, a bottle of wine beneath his arm, Dan kicked the kitchen door of Cassie's house with his toe.

No answer.

"Cassie," he called.

"Come on in. The door's open."

Her voice came, muted by closed windows, from a room he'd never entered. Her bedroom, no doubt. *Don't think about bedrooms, Dan,* he told himself. The mere thought of a bedroom—a bed—with Cassie in it made him ache with wanting her. The Neanderthal in him was closer to the surface than he'd ever realized. It seriously considered bursting in on her, invading her privacy, embracing her with a passion that would sweep aside her last objection. He quelled the thought. He'd promised her time to think, and he meant to let her have it. Balancing the Styrofoam trays on one arm, he opened the back door.

Cassie heard the door open and close and called, "I'll be there in a minute." Or an hour, she thought. Her search for something appropriately seductive to wear had so far been fruitless.

She was being silly; Dan wouldn't give a hoot what she wore. He had made it plain that what he wanted was clothes off, not on. And yet, it mattered to her to be at her most feminine when they first made love.

She shoved hangers to one side. Jeans. More jeans. A couple of tailored dresses she wore when she went to church. And then she saw it. A yellow jumpsuit. Not particularly seductive in itself, but with the zipper at the neck pulled down a few more inches than usual and a pretty patterned scarf as a sash, it would do.

DAN SAT in a straight-backed kitchen chair and waited. He had the wine uncorked and poured, their meals served and on the table, which Cassie had set before he returned. Blunder sat alertly nearby, indicating that he wouldn't be averse to sampling the prime rib or the salmon Dan had brought.

Dan heard footsteps. Then the swinging doors opened to reveal a vision in yellow that dried his mouth and dampened his palms.

The sunny color of the jumpsuit was right for her. Bright and cheerful, like her personality. The fabric molded her hips and hinted at shapely thighs. But Dan's attention was most drawn by the top of the garment. The zipper was open low enough to permit a glimpse of the beginning curve of her breasts. For the first time since he'd met her, she was letting the sensual, seductive woman be clearly seen. Her cheeks were pink, though not from blusher, and her eyes were extra bright.

"Cassie, you look wonderful." His voice was raw with longing.

She looked at Dan. From the moment she first saw him, his face and form had struck chords of response within her. Now she knew more, knew the man himself. He was forceful yet gentle. Kind. Intelligent. She had thought they'd make love after dinner. Now she knew she couldn't wait. She held out her hand and said simply, "Dan."

It was all there in his name, and Dan heard it. Her decision reverberated in that single syllable. He rose and went toward her.

Cassie's heart clamored in her chest as Dan ignored her outstretched hand and cupped her face between his palms. His dark gaze burned into her. "You're sure?" he asked.

She couldn't speak. She nodded and her tongue flicked out to lick her lower lip. The hunger in Dan's eyes seemed to ignite her own desire. As he bent to kiss her, she slid her arms around him, her hands kneading the strong muscles of his back. The kiss deepened; his tongue filled her mouth. He put his arms around her, then dipped his hands lower onto her buttocks to mold her tightly to him.

Their kisses and caresses of the past few days had been leading to this moment. All the desire she had felt for him coiled within her like an over-tightened spring. When the kiss finally ended, she said breathlessly, "My room," then added, "It's just down the hall," as if otherwise he might think they had a long trek before them.

And it seemed an endless journey. In novels, Cassie had noted, couples sometimes seemed to be transported effortlessly into bedrooms. In real life, it seemed a long, long walk, hip bumping hip and their hands on each other.

And in novels, Cassie thought, a man and woman about to make love didn't have an interested dog to contend with. Blunder had followed them, tongue lolling in a doggy smile. She opened her bedroom door. Blunder pushed forward to be the first through. "No!" she said sharply. Then she drew Dan into the room and shut the door, leaving the dog on the other side.

Dan's eyes sparkled with amusement. "Why do I feel guilty that we're shutting him out?"

"I don't know," Cassie said. "I don't feel guilty. Not the slightest bit."

For a moment she feared that the mood had been lost, that now they would be awkward with each other. The scene was not particularly set for passion. Her bed was an old four-poster with a nice firm mattress and a plain blue cotton spread. Extra blankets were piled at the foot. The bed, nightstand, the chest of drawers were all strictly utilitarian.

Then she looked at Dan and the setting no longer mattered. The expression on his face told her he couldn't have desired her more if she'd led him into a courtesan's scented and satined boudoir. She opened her arms to him, and he stepped forward. Embracing her, he lifted her off her feet, then let her slide the length of his body.

Lifting his hands, he slid his fingers through her hair, then kissed her fiercely. She felt his hands trembling as he untied the sash at her waist. Her own fingers were equally unsteady as she unbuttoned his shirt, then pressed her lips to his chest.

Dan stood perfectly still as she eased his shirt off, smoothing her palms over the skin of his shoulders, his back, his upper arms. Then he reached for the zipper tab at the top of her jumpsuit and swept it down past her waist. In a moment she stood proudly before him, clad only in narrow white panties.

Dan gave a low moan as he looked at her. Then he slid her panties down her legs, kneeling, and for a moment his mouth was hot on her inner thigh. Then he stood and began to touch her, caressing her shoulders, breasts, belly, thighs.

Cassie's breath came raggedly. Everywhere he touched, her skin felt hot, as if she must be glowing. She couldn't last much longer standing up. The throb of passion in her lower body was interfering with her legs' ability to hold her upright. But she wanted to see Dan standing before her, as naked as she. Her hands went to his belt.

He smoothed a long caress up her arms as she undid the buckle. But before she could lower his zipper, he dipped his hand into his pocket, then put a foil-wrapped package on the nightstand. Protection, Cassie realized. She hadn't even thought about it. She *should* have thought, she told herself.

And she would think, for the future. Now she could only be grateful that Dan had exhibited more common sense than she.

And then her mind was overwhelmed by a new delight as Dan stepped out of his trousers. The artist in her noted the fine strong lines of his body, the taper of his broad chest to a lean waist and narrow hips, the muscular thighs, the well-made knees and calves. But the woman in her was equally entranced by the part of him that was covered by his dark brown briefs.

Just as he had caressed her, she caressed him now. At first just his chest and arms, then back and buttocks. Then, at last, she eased her fingers beneath the waistband of his briefs and took him in her hand.

It was too much. The shape and hardness of him. His low growl of satisfaction at her touch. Her body was hot and heavy with desire. Too heavy for her to stand up any longer. "Dan . . ." she said, filling the single syllable with her need.

In one swift move, he divested himself of his briefs. A shudder wracked his body as he pulled her tight against him, then drew her down onto the bed. His length pressed against her. His hips moved against hers in the compelling rhythm of passion. Cassie was all sensation. Her breasts felt swollen as she rubbed her tingling nipples back and forth against Dan's chest.

Then he lowered his mouth to her breasts and swept his tongue over her nipples. The heat and wetness flung her onto a new level of desire. A cry broke from her lips, and she opened her legs invitingly. His mouth on her breast, he slid a hand low on her body and found her wet and welcoming. He reached away from her, to the nightstand. In a moment, he was back with her, poised over her.

She reached out a hand to guide him into her. But there was no need. His first thrust was deep and sure, filling her with a pleasure so intense that she felt she might explode. Her hips rose to meet him, pulling him even deeper within her.

"Ah, Cassie." It was a cry of pure passion and pleasure.

Wrought up as they both had been, wanting each other, Dan's rhythmical deep thrusts brought her swiftly to the edge. Shudder after shudder rippled through her, spreading pleasure and completion throughout her body.

Dan was close behind her, with a shout of release. Then he was holding her, his face buried in her throat. "Ah, Cassie," he said again, this time in tones of awe and delight.

A little while later, she lay with his arms around her, her head on his chest. "I can't think why I was so silly," she said.

"Silly?" Dan asked, his voice a soft rumble.

"If I'd had any sense, I'd have dragged you in here that first night you drove me home from the Pizza Bar. Think of all the time we've wasted."

Time. She didn't want to think about time. About how long Dan might stay in Pinetop. At that moment it was easy for her to push the thought aside. There were much nicer things to concentrate on—like the feel of Dan's chest, the hairs damp and crinkly to the touch, the smooth skin over his ribs, the jut of a hipbone.

"Maybe we ought to try to make up for it," he said. "I'm game if you are." As if to demonstrate, he ran his hand down onto her belly, then back up again to cup her breast.

A tingle of renewed desire ran through her. A glance downward showed her that he, too, was feeling new stirrings. She said solemnly, "I certainly think it's worth a try."

It was a try that, in Cassie's estimation, was more than successful. This time, their lovemaking was slower, gentler, a matter of sighs and soft croonings, of touches and caresses, of learning each other's particular pleasures. She discovered where and how, with a touch, she could make Dan tremble; he found the places and pressures that elicited soft moans from her.

But the result was the same—a pleasure and completion so intense that when it was over, Cassie was in a state of delicious liquid bonelessness, like a cat stretched out before a fire.

Thinking of a cat made her remember Dan's tale of his encounter with Tiger, and she smiled to herself, then glanced over at him. His dark lashes were lowered. She whispered, "Are you asleep?"

He shook his head and opened his eyes. "Nope. As a matter of fact, if it's not too crass to mention food at a time like this, I'm hungry. Do you suppose we could reheat those dinners I brought?"

"Dinner!" Cassie gasped. "We left the food on the table, didn't we?"

Dan smiled. "We sure did. As I recall, we got sidetracked." He glanced at Cassie and his smile faded. "What's the matter?"

"Blunder," she said succinctly. "He's a good dog, Dan, but I'm afraid the temptation..."

Moments later, they stood in the kitchen surveying the wreckage of two meals from Pinetop's finest restaurant. A guilty-looking black-and-white dog lay under the table, his head on his paws.

Dan chuckled. "Well," he said philosophically, "at least he didn't drink the wine." He had pulled on his trousers, but was bare-chested. "Don't scold him," he said to Cassie.

"I wasn't going to. It's too late now. But, oh, those lovely meals!"

"Do you have any eggs?"

"Sure."

"Then stand back, lady. I make a mean omelet."

"Terrific!" She took one step toward the refrigerator, then stopped. "Would you mind starting the omelet without me? I'd feel better if I checked on Princess."

"The omelet can wait," Dan said. "Let's both go check on her."

Dressed warmly, Cassie stood outside Princess's stall. Dan was inside, looking the mare over. "She's doing okay," he reported.

He came back out, closing the stall door behind him, then looped his arm around Cassie's waist. Already he was feeling new twinges of desire for her. This insatiability should be no surprise, he thought, considering how much he'd wanted her from the very first. And the reality of making love to her had surpassed even his most fevered imaginings. A fantasy came to him—of making love to her here in the barn in a soft deep pile of hay. Maybe, come summer, they could try it.

A small frown creased his forehead. Come summer, he wouldn't be here, he reminded himself. During the last couple of weeks, he had written letters and made phone calls, sending out feelers for racing work. Next weekend he would go to the track. Make his presence felt. When possible, tell people outright that he was innocent. In time, and with a little effort on his part, he was still convinced the racing fraternity would discover what kind of man Owen Winwood really was.

In time . . . He thought about that for a moment and decided he wouldn't mind too much if it took a while until he could return to the track. Time was what he needed now— for his relationship with Cassie to ripen. When he'd said, out on the mountain, that maybe she would decide to come with him, he had meant it only as a possibility down the line, depending on how things went. Already his feelings had shifted. He couldn't imagine her not being with him, wherever he went when he left here.

He realized she was deeply attached to Pinetop, that the little mountain town was her home, using the word in its most significant sense. But a place was only a place, in Dan's opinion. Already his feelings for Cassie outweighed any question of mere geography. If there'd been a racetrack anywhere near Pinetop where he could have used his skills, he'd have been happy to stay. But there wasn't a track. Never would be. And that meant he had to bank on time deepening and strengthening their relationship to the point that she would leave with him . . . gladly.

He pulled her close against his side. She fit there, he thought. Almost as well as they fit together in bed. "Let's go back inside. I think I may be about to starve to death."

Blunder followed them back into the kitchen. For once in his life, the dog didn't beg for handouts as Dan and Cassie, seated as close together as they could get at the table, feasted on omelets and toast.

9

CASSIE AWOKE to find herself alone in bed. Only the dent in the pillow where Dan's head had lain remained as tangible evidence that they had spent the night together. Then she stretched and discovered that the pillow wasn't quite the only evidence, after all. Her body felt deliciously languid and between her thighs was a pleasant ache of fulfillment. She shook her head in astonished remembrance. After their meal, she and Dan had made love for the third time in a matter of hours. Then they had gone to sleep, wrapped in each other's arms.

She heard a scratching sound and jumped up to open the bedroom door. Blunder gave her an injured look, then backed up, startled, as she enthused, "Oh, Blunder! Isn't it a beautiful day?"

She had just finished the morning feed and was halfway back to the house when the phone began to ring. She dashed to answer it, hoping it would turn out to be Dan. It was, and he said her name with a new intimacy in his voice that made her breath catch in her throat.

"I was just wondering how you were," he said after greeting her.

"Me?" A low laugh bubbled out of her. "I'm terrific! On top of the world. How about you?"

"Just fine. Better than fine," he said warmly, then lowered his voice. "Listen, Cassie. I'm expecting a patient any minute. Or Ellen might come in. So if I change the subject, don't think I've lost my marbles, okay?" Without giving her time to reply, he said, "I just wanted to tell you that last night was . . . indescribable."

"For me, too," she said huskily. Actually she could think of a number of words that described the experience of love-making with Dan pretty well. Glorious and ecstatic were the first to come to mind.

"And leaving you this morning—I hated it. I wanted to wait for you to wake up and then make love to you again, but I thought I'd better go before there was any chance of anyone seeing me leaving."

"About that—" she began, but even through the phone lines, she could hear the tap on Dan's office door.

He called, "Come in," then spoke in a very different voice from the thrillingly intimate one he had used a moment before. "Why, yes," he said. "I ought to be able to stop by later today and have a look at that horse. It's not an emergency, you don't think?"

"*I* have an emergency," she said wickedly. "And you're the doctor with the right medicine for it."

He coughed. "Yes, well, I hope I can take care of it."

"I'm sure you can. Very sure," she said in exaggeratedly throaty tones. She hoped she was driving him crazy. She was driving herself crazy.

"Yes. Well. I'll see you later, then."

"Bye," she said sweetly and hung up the phone. She wondered if he really was planning to stop by or had only said that for the benefit of whomever had entered his office. And she thought about the lengths he had gone to, to keep others from learning that their relationship had entered a new phase. It was nice of him to be so discreet. Totally unnecessary, as far as she was concerned, but nice.

With a smile on her lips and a merry little tune of sheer happiness singing in her heart, she went back outdoors. It was time to muck out the stalls.

IT WAS MID-AFTERNOON before Dan could get away from the office. Half of Pinetop's animals seemed to have developed minor ailments today. He parked his van in the stable yard, then sat behind the wheel for a moment. Cassie was riding Kettle in the arena and apparently hadn't noticed him drive up. As he watched, she eased the horse into a slow canter. The gait remained steady, even on the turns, and Cassie's body moved in perfect rhythm with the horse's stride.

Perfect rhythm. The same that they had found in each other the night before. Instinctively he knew that the way they had been together was something rare, to be cherished and nurtured.

The sight of her body's grace in movement with her horse gave him a new erotic thrill. No time for that, unfortunately. He could only stay for a few minutes.

He got out of the van, took his bag from the back and walked over to the fence. Now Cassie was riding Kettle in slow controlled figure eights. It was a different kind of horsemanship than Dan was used to seeing at the track, but he understood enough about it to appreciate her skill.

He leaned his elbows on the arena fence and waited until she had reined Kettle to a halt before he called, "Hi, there! Mind if I watch for a minute?"

She whipped her head around. "Dan!" she exclaimed. "I didn't hear you drive up." She walked Kettle over to him. "You did come! I didn't know if you really meant it or if you were just saying that."

"I meant it. I hope I'm not interrupting anything."

"You're not. I was just giving Kettle a little exercise." In the sky, dark clouds massed threateningly around Rainbow Peak. Snow was on the way. Tonight or tomorrow, at the latest. Because of it, Cassie'd been working hard to ensure that all the horses got some exercise today.

Kettle was steaming in the cold air. She patted the horse's neck and said apologetically, "I really have to walk him for a little while, to cool him out."

"That's okay. I'll just run in and check Princess. How's she doing?"

"You'll know better than I." Cassie slid off Kettle's back. "But I think she's doing okay. She ate all her mash this morning and a few mouthfuls of hay."

"Great!" He reached across the fence to touch her arm. "How about a kiss?"

She leaned over the fence. Their lips met. What began as a simple kiss of greeting flowered almost instantly into something more intimate. Cassie's tongue boldly probed Dan's mouth. When he finally lifted his head, his breathing was ragged. "Who's going to cool *me* out?" he teased.

As he went off toward the barn carrying his bag, Cassie unsaddled Kettle and put the saddle on the fence, then walked the gelding around the arena. In a little while she heard a cheerfully whistled tune, accompanied by a grating noise, coming from the barn. Dan must be finishing rasping Princess's teeth, she decided.

When Kettle was cool enough to put away, she led the horse into the barn. Dan had Princess tied up in the aisle. "There," he said as Cassie turned Kettle into his stall. "She ought to have an easier time eating now."

She walked over near where he stood at Princess's head. "It was really nice of you to come over to do that, Dan."

He grinned, his eyes twinkling. "That's not why I came over."

"No?"

"Nope. I'm worried about that emergency you mentioned on the phone this morning. I think I might have the same problem you do."

"Really? What are your symptoms? Maybe we should compare."

"Good idea." He loosely encircled her with his arms. "Let's see. My main symptom is that I can't stop thinking about you."

"Oh dear." She pulled a mournful face. "That sounds like exactly the same thing I've got."

Dan lifted a cautioning finger and pressed it to her lips. "Now, let's not be hasty here. That's a pretty general complaint. Maybe we'd better try to be a little more specific."

Cassie lifted her brows. "For instance?"

"For instance..." He pulled her a little closer. "I keep thinking about your mouth."

Cassie nodded. "The very same thing—" Her words were cut off as Dan closed her lips with his own. The kiss quickly intensified. Even with their heavy jackets between them Cassie's body felt as if it were flowing into Dan's, becoming one with him. And the fires he had ignited the night before, she discovered, were only banked, not extinguished, by their lovemaking. New desire sprang to life in her. She twined her arms around his neck, taking this opportunity to feather her fingers through his crisp, soft hair.

A loud throat-clearing coming from the end of the barn penetrated the sensual spell that had Cassie in its grip. Dan seemed to hear the sound at the same moment. He abruptly released her and stepped back, throwing Cassie an apologetic glance.

Dexter Gray, co-owner with Jack of the Pinetop feed and hardware store, stood in the open barn door. "Sorry, folks. Didn't mean to interrupt anything. I guess you didn't hear me drive up."

"I guess not," Cassie said dryly.

The stocky, dark-haired man jerked his thumb over his shoulder. "I've got a load of hay for you, Cass. If the shed's open, I'll start puttin' her in."

"It's open," she confirmed.

Dexter grinned. "I'll get at it then. I wouldn't want to keep you folks from . . . anything. Nice seeing you, Doc."

"Nice seeing you, too, Dexter," Dan said with a noticeable insincerity of tone. He waited until the man had gone, then said with disgust, "That's blown it! And after I was so careful to sneak out of here this morning." He added hopefully, "I don't suppose Dexter's the silent type?"

"'Fraid not. As a matter of fact, he's one of the biggest blabbermouths in town."

Dan grimaced unhappily. "I'm sorry, Cassie."

She looked down at the packed earth floor of the barn. She had started wondering—just a little—why Dan seemed so intent on secrecy. It couldn't be because he was *ashamed* for people to know of their involvement. No, it couldn't, she thought, but the mere possibility made her voice dull. "It's not your fault. And besides, as far as I'm concerned, it's just not a big deal if people know. I mean, I'm not planning to take out an ad in the *Pinecone*, but . . ."

"You don't mind? Really?" There was a note in his voice that made her raise her eyes to meet his.

"No."

"Then there's nothing to worry about, is there?"

"Not a thing." Apart from knowing that, sooner or later, Dan would leave. But she couldn't think about that right now. "Not a thing," she repeated, then added, "unless it bothers *you* that by tonight everybody in town'll have heard that we were making love in the hay."

Dan grinned. The very fantasy that had occurred to him the night before. "Hmm. Might not be a bad idea. It's too cold for it, unfortunately. Maybe when the weather warms up, we can give it a try."

Cassie's heart gave a wild leap. Then she cautioned herself that his remark didn't have to mean anything—that he was planning to stick around until spring, for instance. It was just a remark. She said neutrally, "Maybe. You don't mind that people are going to know about us, then?"

"Mind? Hell, no." A sheepish smile creased his face. "I hate to admit it, Cassie, but I'm afraid I've got a bad case of macho male going here—in addition to that other problem we were discussing. I wouldn't mind the whole world knowing about us." He paused. "Not that I'm going to tell them, of course."

"You won't have to. Dexter'll take care of that." Thumping noises from behind the barn proved that Dexter was unloading bales of hay from his truck into the shed. A gleam came into Cassie's eyes. "That being the case," she suggested, "would you like to adjourn to the house? We could see what we could do about alleviating those symptoms we were discussing." She couldn't believe she was being quite this brazen about expressing her desire. But with Dan it seemed perfectly natural to say what she felt.

He glanced at his watch, then gave her a look filled with dismay. "There's nothing I'd like better. But unfortunately I've got a house call to make...on a pet pig, for heaven's sake."

"Oh, you must be going to the Leaches' place."

"Right. Unfortunately the last time I treated a pig was when I was in vet school. Every minute I had between patients this morning, I spent reading up on porcine diseases." He cocked his head to one side. "Why on earth do the Leaches keep a pig?"

"No one knows," she said darkly. "It's one of the two great mysteries of Pinetop. Maybe you can find out."

"I'll try," Dan promised. He frowned. "What's the other great mystery?"

"Why Adam Benson wears that horrible toupee."

Dan had to smile. He had noticed the man at the Pizza Bar and had wondered why anyone would put what looked like a dead animal on top of his head. He mentally thanked his ancestors for a head of hair that showed no tendency to thin, then said, "I hate like hell to leave, but I guess I'd better get going."

He leaned over and brushed her lips with his. Even such a light, brief contact made Cassie's pulse leap.

As Dan straightened he said, "Say. I have an idea for tonight. Why don't we have that dinner we never got to eat last night?"

"At the Pine Tree?"

He nodded. "And then afterward maybe we can do some scientific experiments."

"Experiments?"

"Sure. Maybe we can come up with a cure for that mutual disease of ours."

"Oh, that." Cassie frowned. "There's just one thing about that, Dan . . ."

"What's that?"

"I'm not sure I really want to be cured."

"Me, neither," he confessed. "But somehow, I don't think that's anything we need to worry about."

She grinned. She wasn't really worried, either. The desire between them was too intense to be slaked in a matter of days . . . or weeks or months, for that matter. Or years? She didn't dare think about years.

She put her fingertips against his chest and gave him a little push. "You'd better go. You wouldn't want to keep the pig waiting."

He was halfway to his van when a sudden recollection made Cassie run after him, calling, "Dan, wait!"

He turned back. "What's the matter?"

"I can't go out to dinner with you tonight. It's the Town Meeting."

THE MEETING HALL was a long low building sandwiched between the movie theater and the Methodist church on Pinetop's principal thoroughfare. Men's and women's clubs as well as the Scouts used the hall for various events, but its essential purpose was to house the monthly gatherings of all Pinetop citizens who were eligible to vote. The town was a true democracy and everyone was allowed to have a say. Sometimes those "says" got loud and lengthy, but usually, in Cassie's opinion, the system worked pretty well.

She arrived a little before seven and parked her truck across the street. Still no snow. It had to come soon, she thought as she thrust her hands deep in the pockets of her down jacket and climbed the steps to the meeting hall.

Others were arriving, and she called friendly greetings to people she had known all her life. She couldn't help wondering to what extent Dexter Gray had already spread the news about her and Dan.

Her question was answered as soon as she entered the foyer of the meeting hall. Mary Jo, a Styrofoam cup of coffee in her hand, took one look at Cassie, then tossed her head and pouted. "Don't you speak to me, Cassie McLean. I'm mad at you."

Cassie knew Mary Jo well enough to know that she wasn't really angry. "Oh? Why's that?"

"You're my best friend," Mary Jo announced, "and I had to hear about you and the doc from my mother."

"It's gotten around already, has it?"

Mary Jo nodded, then said in an awed voice, "Were you really making love right in the middle of the corral? In this weather?"

Good grief! thought Cassie. The tale had gotten even wilder than she'd expected. "No, we were not," she said emphatically. "Not even close. Dexter Gray caught us kissing in the barn, and that's absolutely all."

"Oh." Mary Jo looked disappointed. But then she gave Cassie a cagey look. "Do you mean that's absolutely all that happened, or all that Dexter caught you at?"

Cassie felt a silly, smug smile curving her lips. "Can I take the Fifth on that one?"

"No, you cannot," Mary Jo said indignantly. "And it's too late, anyway. You've as good as answered my question." She grabbed Cassie's hand and pressed it briefly. "I'm really happy for you, Cassie. There's no need to ask how *you* feel about it."

"You mean it shows?"

"Sure, it does. Your eyes are all sparkly." She gave Cassie a frank appraisal. "You look terrific, as a matter of fact. Very... *relaxed*." Mary Jo winked.

"Thanks... I think."

Mary Jo looked around the foyer. "Where is the doc, by the way? I thought he'd probably come with you."

"I invited him," Cassie admitted.

"And?"

"He didn't exactly commit himself." She would see Dan tonight, regardless. They had arranged that she would go to his place afterward if he didn't show up at the town meeting. But she hoped he might decide to attend.

"Well, you can sit with Jack and me, then," said Mary Jo.

"How is it going with you two?"

Mary Jo wrinkled her nose. "Up and down. I—" She broke off as Jack came up beside her.

Town meetings and church were the two places Jack appeared without his cowboy hat. Not wearing it, he looked naked to Cassie. His ears stuck out and were tinged with pink, as if they were embarrassed to be seen without the hat pressed down on them. She'd often wanted to ask Mary Jo if Jack wore the hat in bed, but had never had the nerve.

"Hey, Cassie," Jack said buoyantly. "Say, is it true that you and the doc were—"

Mary Jo elbowed him sharply in the ribs. "No, it's not true, Jack Webley. Dexter's just been making up tall tales again."

Someone called, "Take your seats, folks. Meeting's about to start."

No Dan. So he wasn't coming, after all. Cassie tried to tell herself that it didn't matter. But she kept thinking that if only Dan could *see* the life of the town, as exemplified in the town meetings, he might begin to understand why she felt as she did about this place.

See people losing their tempers or making fools of themselves? Cassie herself could penetrate beyond people's foibles to the pulse of Pinetop life these meetings represented. But would Dan? The point was moot, she thought. He wasn't here.

She followed Jack and Mary Jo into a row of folding chairs near the back of the meeting hall. She was about to take the seat on the aisle, but Mary Jo said to Jack, "Move on over one more, cowboy. We want to leave a seat for the doc."

Cassie shook her head. "I don't think he's coming," she said, trying not to let her disappointment show in her voice.

The mayor, Calvin Engalls, was president of Pinetop's only bank. His passion for hunting and hiking kept him from fitting the portly part of the banker stereotype, but he had the other elements down pat, including a bald head and a pompous manner.

He rapped his gavel for attention. The familiar ritual of the town meeting began. First came the Pledge of Allegiance to the flag that hung on a stanchion near the podium. Then followed the reading of the minutes of the last meeting.

The recording secretary was droning a summary of last month's debate on whether or not to put parking meters on the main street when Cassie felt someone slip into the chair beside her. She turned her head and a bright smile lit up her face when she saw that the newcomer was Dan.

He put his hand on her knee for an instant, the touch of his long fingers immediately working its magic. As he took his hand away, she shifted slightly so her shoulder brushed his and whispered, "I didn't think you were going to come."

"I wasn't," he whispered back. "I was going to catch up on some of the latest vet journals. But I changed my mind."

He wasn't sure why. It would probably be a damned dull couple of hours. But he had told himself that being with Cassie—even in a crowd and where they would have little or no chance to talk—was better than not being with her at all. A little late, he had set out to walk the short distance from Doc Anderson's place.

The minutes read, Mayor Engalls stepped forward once again. "Ladies and gentlemen, I have a matter of some importance to report this evening." He cleared his throat, glanced down at some notes lying on the podium and began in an oratorical voice, "As you all know, Pinetop depends on summer tourists for a considerable percentage of its economic existence."

Several people muttered sarcastically, "Really?" or "Do tell!"

The mayor chose to ignore the comments. "So we are always looking for new ways to attract tourists, yet without losing the unspoiled charm of the village and the beauty of the mountains."

Clem Jones, the owner of the barber shop, snapped, "Get to the point, Your Honor. You're not making a campaign speech."

Dan's eyebrows rose. He whispered to Cassie, "Is this kind of heckling usual?"

"Oh, yes. We always elect Calvin mayor, but we don't let him get away with much."

The mayor shuffled his papers. "We've had a request to waive a zoning ordinance on Rainbow Peak Road." The street was one of the side ones in Pinetop, mostly residential, but with several large empty tracts. "The Partyland chain wants to build a kids' recreational center and pizza parlor. Anyone familiar with those kinds of places?"

Most nodded that they were, but the mayor went on to describe in detail the video games, pinball machines, and giant TV that would be included.

Harry Greville, the owner of the Pizza Bar, waited for the mayor to finish, then said loudly, "It doesn't sound like the kind of thing we want up here."

Mary Jo murmured, "He might not feel that way if Partyland served only hotdogs."

"True," Cassie agreed.

The mayor went on, "Now, Harry, there's something to be said for such a place. Parents could leave their kids there while they're shopping. And that would be good for all the businesses in town."

A woman, one of the most active members of the school board, said, "But do we want *our* kids hanging around a place like that? I've heard of teenagers—elementary school kids, too—turning into video game junkies."

Someone else spoke up, "And wouldn't it attract juvenile delinquents from all over the mountains?"

The mayor said, "That's one of the things we want to find out. Partyland has a place over in Bear Valley. We need to find out what kind of problems may or may not have been created. What we need is a committee to study Partyland's proposal. Do I have any volunteers?"

Harry Greville jumped to his feet. "I volunteer."

The mayor shook his head. "Now, Harry, I'm afraid we'll have to disqualify you. I think everyone knows how you'll vote on the issue."

"Aw, okay." Harry reluctantly sat back down. "Partyland's pizzas aren't any good, anyway."

Someone called, "How do you know? Have you ever tried one?"

"They couldn't be as good as mine," Harry said stoutly. "It's impossible!"

The mayor gaveled for silence. "Any other volunteers for the committee?"

A couple of people raised their hands and were duly appointed. Then the mayor said, "We need at least one more. Come on, folks. Where's your sense of civic duty?"

Dan leaned closer to Cassie. "Aren't you going to volunteer?"

She shook her head. "Not me. I'm on two committees already."

"How about nominations from the floor, then?" the mayor suggested.

Two seats down, Jack raised his hand. "I nominate the new doc. Doc Faraday."

Dan jerked in his seat. His mouth opened, and Cassie was certain he was going to refuse. It shouldn't matter, she told herself. He had every reason not to want to get involved. It would mean trips over to Bear Valley to check out the Partyland facility there, talks with Partyland execs and, most likely, plenty of arguments with his fellow committee members.

"Doc?" The mayor looked at Dan. "How about it?"

He hesitated for what seemed to Cassie like eons. "Okay," he said at last.

She felt the air whoosh out of her lungs. Surely his acceptance was a sign, a portent for the future. He wouldn't have agreed if he was planning to take off next week or next month, would he?

The mayor thumped the lectern with his gavel. "That's the committee, then." He read off Dan's name and the two others. "All right. You folks get together and pick a time for your first meeting. Next order of business . . ."

At a little before nine, Mayor Engalls gaveled for the last time. "Meeting adjourned."

Everyone stood. Holding his hat in his hands, Jack moved closer to Dan. "I hope you're not too mad at me, Doc," he said sheepishly.

"I ought to be," Dan said, "but I'm not. It's okay."

"I just thought you were the best man for the job," Jack explained. "I figured you'd see through it if those Partyland guys try to pull any wool over folks' eyes. Being from the city and all."

Dan didn't altogether understand Jack's reasoning, but he said, "Well, I'll do my best."

Several other people came up to talk. A moment later, Dan was drawn into a huddle with his fellow committee members. When he finally broke away, he found Cassie in the foyer, talking to a couple of other women. The pair said hello—with knowing expressions on their faces that proved that, as Cassie had predicted, the whole town now knew of their relationship.

"Sorry to keep you waiting," he said to Cassie as soon as the other women had departed. He looked around. "Did Jack and Mary Jo leave? I thought the four of us might go get a beer at the Pizza Bar."

"That's funny," Cassie said. "They suggested the same thing, and I told them no."

"Did you? Why?"

"I didn't know if you'd want to or not."

He gazed seriously at her. "I would have liked it. Not that I wouldn't prefer being alone with you. But I'd like to get to know your friends."

Her smile seemed to come up from the tips of her toes. "We'll do it some other time," she said. More and more, it looked as if there would be time for such things. And the way Dan was fitting into her life—especially the way he seemed to *enjoy* fitting in—tickled her pink.

She let her hand slip into his as they crossed the foyer. Fingers linked, they stepped outside into a Christmas card. "Oh, look!" Cassie cried. "It's snowing."

"SO WHAT DID YOU THINK of the town meeting?"

Cassie and Dan were sitting in her kitchen, sipping hot chocolate. They had come back to her place after a swift trip to Dan's house for a razor and clean clothes for the morning.

"Interesting," he said noncommittally.

She looked into her cup. "I was kind of surprised when you let yourself get dry-gulched into being on that committee."

"I was a bit surprised myself," he admitted. Dan honestly had no idea why he hadn't declined. He had been aware of people's eyes on him, people who had welcomed him warmly into the community. It would have been ungrateful to refuse, he had told himself.

But there had been something else. He had sensed Cassie beside him, sending out vibrations, *willing* him to agree to serve. Weird, he thought. He was starting to feel sometimes as if he could read her mind. He hadn't liked the idea of disappointing her . . . even though he had no idea why it should matter to her so much.

"I don't know," he said lightly. "It seemed like the thing to do."

Because you're getting involved, Cassie thought triumphantly. *Because you're coming to see what life in a close-knit community like this can mean—friends and neighbors all helping one another. Because, whether you know it or not, somewhere in the back of your mind, you're starting to think you might stay.*

Or else she was indulging in a full-blown case of wishful thinking again. Which, given her natural tendencies, might well be the case, she cautioned herself.

She looked up to find Dan gazing at her with a light in his dark eyes that made her heart thump an extra beat. "Tired?" he asked softly.

"Not really."

"Me, either." He paused. "Since neither of us is tired, why don't we go to bed?"

Cassie grinned. "I like your logic, mister."

DAN LAY ON HIS SIDE holding Cassie in his arms, spoon-fashion. She was drowsy, replete, but the memory of their lovemaking still sang in her veins, like the echoes of a lovely melody.

Dan's breath stirred her hair. "I have to tell you something, lady."

He paused, but before she could even begin to worry that what he had to say was something dreadful—that he was leaving Pinetop, for instance—he went on. "I think I'm falling in love with you, Cassie."

Joy welled up in her, happy tears pooling in her eyes. It didn't matter that it had already gone much farther than that with her. She wasn't *starting* to fall in love. She *was* in love.

With that realization came a little jolt. She hadn't formed the thought before. Not in actual words. And yet, now that she *had* thought it, she knew it was true and had been true, at least for a while.

It was odd that she couldn't pinpoint the exact moment when it had happened. Maybe it had been when they made love for the first time. Or perhaps before that, when she saw his tender concern for Princess, so different from the sleek Thoroughbreds he was accustomed to, yet, apparently, in his eyes, worthy of every ounce of his dedication and skill.

Or maybe she'd fallen in love with him the first moment she saw him at the Pizza Bar. Yes, now that she thought about it, she'd been a goner from that instant. Her feeble attempts to evade and avoid him had had no more substance than dandelion fluff in a heavy gale.

Whenever it had happened didn't matter now, she decided. She was in love with Dan Faraday. Deeply. Truly. What would happen to them from here, she couldn't guess, could hardly bear to think about. But at this moment, even that didn't matter compared to her realization of how she felt.

She turned her head to tell him that she loved him, but his eyes were closed and he was breathing deeply, his arms still wrapped around her, his lean hard body pressed close to hers.

She smiled ironically into the darkness. So much for her heartfelt declaration. The man she loved was fast asleep.

10

THE LUNCHTIME CROWD at the Koffee Kup Kafe filled no more than half the booths. Cassie sat at one across from Mary Jo, next to a window that looked out onto the street. Icicles dripped from the eaves of the shops across the way. More snow was predicted for later in the week, but the last few days had been sunny and clear.

Inside, Cassie felt even sunnier than the weather. In the last three weeks, since she and Dan had become lovers, she had experienced a springtime flowering of happiness.

She finished her last bite of pie and shoved the plate aside. "Okay, Mary Jo, don't you think it's about time you told me why you wanted to have lunch?"

Mary Jo arched her brows. "Why, Cassie! You're my best friend. Why shouldn't we have lunch?"

"Of course, we can have lunch," Cassie said patiently. "Anytime. But when you called, you said it had to be today. Not tomorrow. Not next week. Then I get here and you talk about the weather, you talk about clothes, you talk about your job at the phone company. You talk about everything, but none of it sounds very urgent to me. Not the way you sounded on the phone."

Mary Jo leaned across the table. In a voice barely above a whisper, she said, "I have to talk to you. But not here. Someone might overhear us."

Cassie glanced around. "For heaven's sake, Mary Jo! Two booths on either side of us are empty. Who's going to overhear?" She looked at her friend's stricken expression and said, "Oh, all right. We'll take a walk. How's that?"

The crusty snow piled in ridges by the side of the road crunched under their boots as the two women walked past the gift shop and the bakery. Several fellow Pinetoppers called greetings, but in a matter of minutes, they were out of the town proper, on a narrow road that led only to a few scattered cabins.

Cassie said, "Okay, we're alone. What's the matter, Mary Jo?"

"A couple of days ago, Jack asked me to marry him."

"Mary Jo!" Cassie beamed delightedly at her friend. "You told him yes, didn't you?"

Mary Jo shook her head. "I told him I needed some time to think about it."

Cassie thought of poor Jack, wondering and waiting. She could empathize with him. Though her days—and especially her nights with Dan—were filled with joy, underneath was a layer of tension. It was true that Dan had said nothing lately about leaving Pinetop. But neither had he so much as hinted that he might be considering staying permanently. He said he was in love with her; he said he was crazy about her, that he couldn't get enough of her. But he never said he wanted to make her life his life and plan a future for them both in the town she loved.

And then there were those trips of his to L.A. Two of them in the last couple of weeks...

She looked at Mary Jo. "What *are* you going to tell Jack?"

Mary Jo bit her lip. "I just don't know." She walked on a few steps, then stopped to scuff at a small mound of snow. "I *think* I'm in love with him."

Mary Jo didn't sound too sure, Cassie noticed. Nowhere near as certain as she was about her own feelings for Dan.

"It's just . . . if I marry him, we'll stay right here in Pinetop, for our whole lives."

"Is that so awful?"

"Yes. No. I don't know." Mary Jo hugged herself. "Oh, Cassie, I'm so confused."

Cassie put her hand on her friend's shoulder. "Have you told Jack how you feel?"

"How can I? You know Jack. He's just like you. He thinks Pinetop's the greatest. He's got his business. His cabin. He wouldn't understand . . ." She looked Cassie full in the face. "You know something? It should have been *you* and Jack. The two of you could have settled down here in Pinetop and been perfectly happy."

"But Jack didn't fall in love with me. He fell in love with you." She didn't think it necessary to add that, even though he was one of her dearest friends, never in a million years could she have fallen for Jack.

"I know. But it just seems that things work out all wrong sometimes. Just think about it, Cassie. Here you are, in love with a man who, sooner or later, is going to leave Pinetop . . . the very thing I want to do most in the whole world."

Cassie tried to keep the tightness from her voice. "What makes you so sure Dan's going to leave?"

Mary Jo gazed at her with an expression of mild astonishment. "Well, his taking over for Doc Anderson has always been just temporary, hasn't it? Besides, I heard that Doc Anderson offered Dan a chance to buy the practice, and Dan turned him down."

"I know. Clem Jones said something about that a while back." She knew that Dan's refusal hadn't been for financial reasons. He had told her how fortunate he had been with his investments. And Doc Anderson, she was pretty sure, would have offered reasonable terms.

"You haven't talked to Dan about it?"

"Not really." She paused. "He could always change his mind. Doc Anderson still doesn't have anyone else lined up to buy the practice, as far as I know." Knowing she was searching desperately for reasons to hope, she said, "And besides, look at the way Dan's gotten involved in town business. He's spent lots of time doing stuff for that committee he's on."

She knew she was emphasizing the positive; and there was that big negative she didn't feel like mentioning to Mary Jo. Twice, now, Dan had spent Sunday in L.A. He'd said he had business to take care of at the Santa Theresita track, where he used to work. Dull business, he'd explained, that would take all day. And he hadn't invited her to go with him.

Her feelings on the subject were so mixed that it had taken her several days to sort them out. On the one hand, she trusted Dan completely. There was no woman but her in his life, not even the remnant of a previous relationship. So she had no cause for jealousy.

But she *hated* his trips to Los Angeles. It seemed a sign that he was still tied to the city and his former life. The thought of that tie one day drawing him back, taking him away from her, made her stomach hurt.

Mary Jo was eyeing her closely. "Are you okay, Cassie?"

"Fine. Just fine."

"Sure you are. Just like I'm fine about Jack and me." Mary Jo put her hand on Cassie's arm. "Look, you're the one who usually gives *me* advice, but let me just turn it around for once. Instead of eating yourself up wondering, why don't you just ask Dan what his plans are?"

"Maybe I will."

"And maybe you won't, because you don't want to know the answer." Mary Jo gave her an earnest look. "I probably shouldn't say this, but I think you're kidding yourself, Cassie. At least I'm realistic about Jack. I'm not trying to make myself believe that things are going to be exactly the way I want them to be."

Was she kidding herself? Cassie wondered. Did all the positive signs really mean nothing? Not only was Dan involved in town affairs, but he fitted in with her friends, and when he spoke of his work here in Pinetop, it was with enthusiasm. What were a couple of little trips to L.A. against all of that?

But thinking of those trips made a darkness spread through her mind. In an effort to lighten it, she said abruptly, "Hey! How'd we get off onto me and Dan? It's you and Jack we're supposed to be talking about."

"You're right. So, what do you think I should do?"

"I can't decide for you. But I think you should explain to Jack exactly how you feel. Then at least he'd understand why you're having trouble making up your mind."

Mary Jo was silent for a moment. "All right. I'll do that. I'll tell him tonight." She cocked her head to one side. "And maybe you ought to have a heart to heart with Dan, too."

"Maybe," Cassie admitted. "I'll think about it."

IT WAS WARM in Cassie's kitchen. Blunder lay stretched out near the stove. The dinner dishes were soaking in the sink and a chessboard sat in the middle of the table. Cassie and Dan had discovered a mutual enthusiasm for the game. She had played often with her father during his last years; Dan, it turned out, had belonged to the chess club in high school.

Most times they played, they were a fairly even match. But not tonight. Dan had won the first game and, although she had vowed revenge, Cassie's mind hadn't been on the second game, either. Dan had taken her pieces as easily as he had captured her heart.

He advanced a knight into the middle of her severely depleted forces. "Checkmate!"

"No!" Cassie protested, but a brief study of the board showed that her king was trapped. "Okay. You win...again."

Dan eyed her closely. "That was an awfully easy win. You must not have been paying attention."

It was the perfect opening. She could say, "I was thinking about something else," and when he asked her what, she could tell him she'd been wondering about his plans.

She looked at his face. Though portrait painting was not her forte, she had done dozens of sketches of him in recent weeks. His eyes. His mouth. The line of his jaw. All were as familiar to her now as her own features...and infinitely dear. She said, "I was thinking that Princess seems well enough that she might be able to go down the hill to pasture soon. What do you think?"

"Should be okay. I'll take a look at her in the morning."

"If she's all right, I'll trailer her down some time in the next day or two." She was talking about this trivial matter, because she didn't want to say what was really on her mind, she realized. Obviously, Mary Jo was right. She didn't want to know the truth.

Cassie had heard a saying once: "Never ask a question if you can't handle the answer." That seemed right to her and applicable to this case. If Dan told her he was leaving on a certain date—or even at some unspecified but roughly foreseeable point in the future—it would spoil everything for her. *Get the happiness while you can, Cassie,* she thought. How foolish it would be to toss away such a valuable and rare commodity as the joy she was experiencing with Dan.

He glanced at the board. "Another game?"

"I don't think so. Unless you want to."

He grinned. "I can think of a game I'd rather play."

To tease him, she pretended not to understand. "Oh, well, if you're tired of chess, I think I have a Monopoly set around somewhere."

"Not Monopoly."

"Gin rummy? I'm sure I have a deck of cards."

He was leaning farther and farther across the table, a humorous glint and the spark of desire in his dark eyes. "I hate gin rummy. Think of something else."

"Crazy Eights? Old Maid? Go Fish?"

As she spoke, he rose and came around the table. Bending, he tipped her face up and kissed her thoroughly.

"Oh, *that* game," Cassie said when he released her. "My favorite."

"Mine, too," he said with a new huskiness in his voice.

With Dan's arm around her shoulders, hers around his waist, they started toward the bedroom. Halfway through the living room, Dan paused.

It actually surprised him that he noticed the new acrylic hanging above the chintz couch. His desire for Cassie continued unabated, and his mind—with marked effects on his physical condition—was already engaged in making love to her. But there it was, something new she must have painted during the past few days, and it captured his attention.

It was more abstract than the painting of the horse now hanging in his office, more abstract than anything of hers he'd seen. To the casual eye, it was only shapes and colors. A slant of tawny gold. A curve of peach. A sharper line of rich, deep brown. Yet, he saw in the elusive and illusive shapes a man and woman locked in a passionate embrace.

"That's wonderful, Cassie," he said sincerely. "Do you have a name for it?"

She shook her head. "I don't usually bother with titles."

"This one should be called *The Lovers*."

Cassie turned to look at him, smiling. "You figured it out. I didn't think anyone would."

"Of course, I did." He squeezed her shoulder, then said urgently, "Don't sell it, Cassie."

"I wasn't planning to."

The relief Dan felt was overwhelming. For her to sell that picture would be like selling part of them. He visualized it hanging in a bedroom in a house he and Cassie shared. Where that house would be, he couldn't guess. Somewhere near a track or, perhaps, close to a concentration of Thoroughbred breeding farms. Eventually he was bound to get back into racing. Owen Winwood's credibility couldn't last forever.

But it was lasting longer than he'd thought it would. His trips to the Santa Theresita track—to show his face, let his presence be felt and see how the wind was blowing, in his favor or against—had been unpleasant. Fear that they would turn out that way was what had kept him from inviting Cassie along. He hadn't wanted her exposed to the kind of potentially ugly scene that had taken place on his first visit, when he encountered a group of owners and trainers in the clubhouse bar. One of them, a big, red-faced man who'd obviously had a few drinks too many had sneered visibly at Dan, then said loudly, "Look what they're letting in these days, fellas. Ought to do something about that."

The others, reputable horsemen all, had shushed their colleague. When it became obvious that Dan had no intention of retreating, they had surrounded the red-faced man like a pack of trained dogs encircling an unruly sheep and had herded him away. And not one of those men had said a word to Dan, or even made eye contact with him.

Dan had only seen Owen Winwood, the engineer of his disaster, from a distance. He hadn't dared go closer for fear of giving in to his anger and smashing Winwood's face in.

But even after all of that, he had faith in the essential justice and fairness of the racing world. Sooner or later Winwood would be seen for what he was and Dan's name would be cleared. Then there could be that house where Cassie's painting could hang and where she would share his bed...and his life. But for now, he was in no position to mention it.

Cassie looked at Dan. He was still gazing at the painting, silent, as if enthralled. Impulsively, she said, "If you really like it so much, it's yours."

If worse came to worst, it would be something for him to remember her by, she thought. She wouldn't need anything to keep her memories of him alive. And the years ahead—if they should be years without Dan Faraday in her life—looked more bleak than the desert lands down the mountain.

Don't think about it, she instructed herself. *Don't borrow trouble.*

She didn't understand why he scowled. And the scowl disappeared so quickly, she thought she might have imagined it.

"I love the painting," he said. "As far as your giving it to me goes..." He shrugged. "We'll talk about that some other time."

Didn't he want the painting? she wondered. Why not? He had said he liked it...

Something dark seemed to hover in the air between them, emanating from each of them. She knew what it was, on her side of things. The question she was afraid to ask refused to disappear completely. It was still there, lurking at the back of her mind.

What was bothering Dan, though, she couldn't guess. Something about her painting must have triggered it, but what? Should she ask, try to force him to tell her? Would it help or would it hurt? Maybe she ought to let *him* choose the time.

The decision was made for her. Dan pulled her tight against his side. He bent to nuzzle her neck, and his breath was warm against her ear as he said in a lighthearted voice, "Hey! I thought we were going to play our favorite game." His tone, his embrace, clearly told her that, whatever his problem, he didn't want to discuss it right now.

With a vast feeling of relief, Cassie responded in kind. "Speaking of games, Dan, have I got news for you!"

"What's that?"

"You were the big winner at chess tonight, right?"

"Mmm-hmm." His lips were pressed against her throat.

"Well, I'm pleased to announce that you've won a prize."

"As far as I'm concerned, I've already got the prize." He turned slightly so his arms were around her. "Right here."

He pulled her closer. With a little sigh of pleasure, Cassie let her lower body press against his. "But this is an extra-special prize." She wasn't allowed to explain. Dan's mouth claimed hers, and the familiar heat spread through her as she clung tightly to him.

But it was in the same spirit of determined lightheartedness that she said to Dan a few minutes later, "You don't seem very interested in finding out about that special prize you won."

"Oh, right. I remember now. What prize was that?" He had stripped to his shorts and was sitting on the edge of the bed.

She, similarly unclothed, stood next to him. Spreading her arms wide, she said, "Ta-dah! Your own personal love slave, reporting for duty."

"Wow!" Dan's grin lit up his face. Whatever worry had shadowed his eyes earlier was gone now, she was pleased to see. "If I'd known *that* was the prize, I'd have tried even harder to win."

Refusing to consider any possible similarity between her own determined gaiety and Nero reaching for his fiddle, she poked his chest with one finger. "Lie down, oh master!"

He caught her hand and kissed her fingertip. "Wait a minute! I thought you were the slave. How come you're giving the orders?"

"Because that's the kind of slave I am. Lie down, or you'll be sorry. I'm warning you."

"Oh, yeah?"

"Yeah!" said Cassie and lunged for his ribs.

They grappled, laughing and protesting, pretending to try to tickle each other, until they ended up on the bed in a tangle of arms and legs.

"Give up?" Cassie asked, though there was no particular reason Dan should. He had the advantage. By now, what had begun as artificial playfulness was feeling real to her. She had thought about what she was planning to do *to* Dan and *with* Dan, and it sounded absolutely wonderful.

"I surrender," he said, then slid his hands down the side of her body, his mouth coming to hers.

"Oh no!" Cassie wriggled out of his grasp and knelt beside him. "You're supposed to just lie there, remember? And let your slave minister to your every wish."

"My *every* wish?"

"You got it."

"What if my wish is to . . ." He completed his sentence wordlessly by caressing her breast.

"Not fair," Cassie said, though the thrill of his touch made her momentarily regret the rules she had mentally established for the love-slave game. "Your role is strictly to lie there and be . . . uh, masterful."

"In a passive sort of way?"

"Exactly."

He lay back on the pillow. "I'll try," he said dubiously. "It may be tough."

He did surprisingly well, she thought a little time later. He let her caress him without reaching for her. Cassie used light touches at first, merely brushing his skin and teasing the fine dark hair on his chest and legs. But then, gradually increasing the pressure of her fingers, she began straying more frequently to his lower body, to touch and rub his jutting erection. His hands lifted, moving toward her, and she saw the willpower it took for him to force his arms back down to his sides.

And she was cheating, she realized. She was supposed to be ministering to Dan's desire, but her own was being very effectively aroused in the process. She could feel her nipples tingling and the moisture gathering between her thighs.

He wouldn't be able to hold out much longer, she thought, hearing the soft sounds wrenched from him by her increasingly passionate caresses. Nor would she. It was getting difficult to concentrate on pleasing Dan with her own body craving release.

Just one more thing . . .

She slid down the bed so her mouth was level with his hips. His erection was fully extended, standing straight up from its nest of dark hair. She closed her lips over the smooth tip, wetting him thoroughly with her tongue.

Dan's groan sounded almost painful. And Cassie's own response was equally intense. Inside, she was throbbing, aching with the need for him to fill her.

She sat up and straddled him, then lowered herself onto his body. Dan lifted his hips, sheathing himself deep within her.

It was a wild ride he took her on. Though tonight her role was the aggressor's, it was he who found and established their mutual rhythm—a steady tempo, at first, with deep penetrating thrusts.

The speed of their movements increased. Dan reached down and grasped her buttocks. Cassie's eyes were wide open, but she saw nothing. All of her awareness was focused on the feel of him inside her. The jolts of sensation came faster and faster, sliding together to become an unrelenting heat. Her head tossed and she forgot to breathe. Her teeth clamped together and her short blunt nails bit into Dan's arms as she was shaken by an intense convulsion of pleasure. She cried out, a high wavering cry, and heard Dan's own hoarse shout of release virtually in unison with hers.

She collapsed limply onto his damp chest. When his breathing had slowed and her lungs, too, were working more normally, she eased herself over to lie beside him. In awed tones, she said, "By golly! Do you know what that was?"

Dan nodded and put his arms around her, drawing her close. "A simultaneous orgasm, I believe it's called."

"I thought that was a myth."

"Apparently not." He kissed her forehead, then her eyelids. After a while, he said, "If you think of it, Cassie, remind me there's a book I want to order from the book store."

"What's that?"

He chuckled. *"How to Play Winning Chess."*

"IS HE GOING to be all right, Doc?"

"He's going to be just fine," Dan said soothingly. He was stitching up a dachshund while the dog's anxious owner looked on. The dachshund, with delusions of grandeur, had attacked a Doberman.

He had only a few stitches to go when Ellen knocked on the treatment room door. "Doc Anderson on the phone. Can you talk to him now or should I take a message?"

"Tell him I'll get back to him in five minutes." He took the last stitch, then handed the dog over to its owner.

Mr. Sloan, an elderly man with a grim Winslow Homer face, cradled the dog in his arms and said surprisingly, "Is oo okay? Did that nasty beast hurt my 'ittle Snookums?" Then, to Dan, he said briskly, "Anything in particular I should do for him, Doc?"

"Don't let him run around loose for a while," Dan said, hiding a smile. "And you might try to convince him that he'd be better off picking on someone his own size."

"I'll do that," Mr. Sloan said seriously. "We'll have a little talk about it on the way home."

People and their pets, Dan thought, mentally shaking his head in wonder as he showed Mr. Sloan out of the treatment room. It was a slice of life he wouldn't have seen if he'd kept on working only with racehorses, and he was finding it fascinating.

Not that some of the owners he'd known at the track hadn't had a personal relationship with their horses. But it wasn't the same. A racehorse couldn't sleep on its owner's bed—as he suspected was the case with Mr. Sloan and "Snookums."

He crossed the hall to his office, sat down behind his desk, and dialed Doc Anderson's number. "Hi, Doc! How are you?"

"Just fine, Dan. How's it going up the mountain?"

Knowing the older man would enjoy them, he related a few anecdotes from his past few weeks of work. Doc Anderson laughed heartily when Dan explained how he had finally managed to examine Tiger. Having spotted the biggest, toughest high school kid in town, he had offered the boy ten dollars for twenty minutes work. The boy, outfitted in protective clothing, including a face mask like a goalie's and thick leather gloves had held onto Tiger while Dan examined the cat.

"Clever," Doc Anderson said admiringly. "I never thought of that. I always had to come up with some excuse why Mrs. Carmichael had to leave Tiger overnight. Then I'd sedate him. She would have had a fit if she'd known." He cleared his throat. "The reason I called was to tell you that there's a fellow interested in buying the practice."

"Oh?" Dan's voice was noncommittal, but he felt a pang of dismay. He'd hoped to be back in racing by the time Doc Anderson had found a buyer. But the main reason he was unhappy to hear the news was because of Cassie. He'd also hoped for a little more time for their relationship to mature before he asked her to leave Pinetop with him.

Holding the phone, he realized there was no longer the slightest question in his mind that that was what he wanted. He simply couldn't imagine life without her.

He felt a little guilty that he had never mentioned to Cassie Doc Anderson's earlier offer to sell him the practice and his refusal. It was partly because the subject had never come up, and partly because he didn't want to rock the boat.

Doc Anderson gave Dan the prospective buyer's name—Kevin Ohlson—which Dan dutifully wrote down. Then the older man said, "He wants to come up and take a look around sometime soon. I thought I ought to give you a little warning." He paused, then added hopefully, "You haven't changed your mind, have you, Dan?"

"No. No, I haven't."

"Too bad. I thought you might have. I hear you've gotten pretty involved up there . . . in more ways than one. Between that pretty little McLean girl and the way you've gotten mixed up in town affairs."

Obviously Doc Anderson was keeping abreast of Pinetop news. Dan made a noncommittal sound.

Doc Anderson sighed regretfully. "In any case, if Ohlson does decide to buy the practice, he's flexible about when he takes over. You'll have a little leeway to make your own plans."

"Thanks," Dan said. "I appreciate that." He had a hunch that Ohlson's flexibility might have been at Doc Anderson's insistence.

After the phone call ended, Dan sat for a moment, frowning thoughtfully. He'd vowed to make another visit to his former world this weekend. He couldn't see that going to the track was doing him much good—the silent, unfightable blacklist against him was still in effect. Yet he couldn't just give up. Disappear.

But he hated the idea of spending another whole day away from Cassie. Then an idea came to him. Why not invite her to go with him? Racing at Santa Theresita was over now. This weekend they were running at Los Angeles Park. Away from his home track, there would be only a slight risk of exposing Cassie to an unpleasant scene.

Why not? he thought. They could make a day of it. The races. Dinner some place both elegant and fun. Maybe a show, if he could get tickets. He hadn't really had a chance to spoil her as he would have liked to, as he'd thought of doing the first night they met. At least he could give her a wonderful day—and work on his professional problems at the same time.

He checked his appointment book. No patients after three. He picked up the phone and dialed Cassie's number.

HUMMING HAPPILY to herself, Cassie came out the back door of her house with Blunder following along behind. She was on her way to the barn to tack up Kettle and King. Dan had called a little while before to say that he had some free time that afternoon; how would she like to go for a ride?

It was a perfect day to be on horseback. The sun was shining. In the shadows of the trees snowdrifts still lay deep, but the temporary thaw had cleared the roads and wider dirt tracks.

Earlier in the day Mary Jo had called to say that she'd had that chat with Jack. He had seemed to understand the reasons for her indecision, Mary Jo had said, and had promised to give her time to think. Fortunately, Mary Jo hadn't asked if Cassie had been similarly forthright with Dan.

She pushed that thought away to concentrate on a more pleasant topic. That morning before leaving, Dan had pronounced Princess fit enough to go to pasture. Tomorrow or the next day, Cassie planned to drive the mare down the mountain in her horse trailer. It was about time to visit the pastured horses, anyway. The owner of the land checked them daily when he brought hay to supplement the sparse winter grasses, but Cassie liked to see for herself how they were doing.

She was next to the corral fence when Blunder let out a startled woof and a figure stepped out of the shadows at the corner of the barn. It was Willie, looking scruffier, if that was possible, than the last time she'd seen him.

"Willie! What are you doing here?"

He straightened drooping shoulders and said with attempted bravado, "I'm back, Cassie. I'll be able to work for you this winter, after all."

He must not have found work so easy to get in Palm Springs, she thought. She moved closer to the old man and immediately regretted it. Whatever Willie had been doing for the past month, it was obvious he hadn't been near a bathtub or a shower.

"It's nice to see you, Willie." She went on, determined to be firm, "But I'm afraid there's a little bit of a misunderstanding here. There really isn't enough for you to do in the winter, with most of the horses gone."

"There's still stalls to clean, aren't there?"

"Well, sure, but . . ." She bit her lip. She felt sorry for the old man, but her budget wouldn't allow her to feel *too* sorry for him. "I'm afraid I just can't afford to pay you. Not in the wintertime."

A spasm of anger contorted his grizzled features. "I guess I know when I'm not wanted."

The old man's pride must have been pretty badly hurt down the mountain for him to be so touchy, Cassie thought. She said, "Wait a minute, Willie. There's no need for you to leave right this minute. I could fix you a sandwich, if you want. And . . ." She paused, not knowing how to put it delicately. "If you'd like to clean up a little, you can use the bathroom in the house." She wouldn't think about the state it would be in when he was done.

He scowled furiously. "I don't need no charity from you." With a jerk of his head, he turned his back on her.

Feeling perplexed and guilty, Cassie watched as Willie's shambling strides took him across the stable yard and onto the highway.

"I HAVE AN IDEA," Dan said.

Kettle and King walked side by side on a fire road that wound through a stretch of woods near town. Summer cabins peeked through the trees. A rabbit, wearing its winter coat, gave a startled leap and bounded for cover with Blunder chasing after.

"He won't catch it," Cassie said, in case Dan was worried about the rabbit's fate. "He never does. What's your idea, Dan?"

"It depends on whether you can get away on Sunday."

"No problem," she said promptly. Jennifer would be happy to feed the horses and keep an eye on things. "What do you have in mind?"

"I need to go down the mountain again this weekend. To the races at Los Angeles Park. I'd like you to go with me. Afterward, we'll go out to dinner. Maybe a show or something."

"You mean go all the way to L.A.?"

Dan's mouth quirked with amusement. She sounded as if he were proposing an expedition to Borneo. "It's only a three-hour drive."

Cassie shifted uncomfortably in the saddle. She'd hoped these visits of his to L.A. were over. Obviously not. But maybe, there at the track, he would explain why he kept going back. It could be some perfectly innocuous reason, she thought hopefully. Nothing that would eventually take him away from her.

And it occurred to her that maybe at the races she'd find out why he'd looked so pained and angry—especially when he first came to Pinetop—at every mention of his former work. She wanted to know everything about him, except for that one little thing she definitely *didn't* want to know—if he was leaving Pinetop anytime in the near future.

She drew a deep breath. "Sure, Dan. That sounds like fun."

11

A BRIGHT, HOT SUN glittered on acres of parked cars. Though it had only been a few years since her last visit, Cassie had forgotten how many people there were everywhere you went in L.A.—people you didn't know and who didn't know you. Although anonymity might be nice sometimes, the idea of it as a way of life appalled her.

But the sun felt good. Up in Pinetop, there had been fresh snow falls and frigid nights. It was a treat not having to bundle up. And since Dan obviously wanted her to enjoy herself today, Cassie was determined to have fun.

Banners flying on tall poles around the entrance snapped in the breeze as Dan paid their admission, and he and Cassie passed through the turnstile.

Dan drew a deep breath. He wanted to show Cassie a good time, but he had to remember that he was there for a reason.

He glanced at her as they walked with the flow of the crowd toward the entrance to the stands. She looked pretty—and citified—in a dark-green-and-white print dress with long sleeves and a full skirt that swirled around her knees. She was even wearing high heels. The lady had terrific legs, he thought, though he appreciated them even more when they were naked and wrapped around him.

Business aside, he wanted to give her a wonderful day. First the races, then the show, currently the hottest attraction in L.A., with dinner in between at one of his favorite restaurants. She deserved these little luxuries. In fact, she deserved nothing but the good things in life, and it was his intention to do everything he could to see she got as many of them as he could give her.

"It's nearly an hour until the first race," he said. "Buy you a sandwich?"

"Sounds good to me."

They went through a tunnel that brought them into the open-air midway up the stands. Below was the oval track, empty now, and the board that would flash the odds before each race and announce the winners once the horses had crossed the finish line.

Dan led Cassie up the steps. Higher up, an archway opened onto an area inside the stands that had betting windows on one wall, a fast-food counter on the other.

Dan ushered Cassie past the people already lining up to place their bets. At a doorway, a guard checked a card Dan took from his pocket before letting them pass into the club-house.

As they entered, Dan glanced around the room. He expected to find people there he knew. The clubhouse was the hangout for the trainers, owners...and veterinarians, for that matter. He wasn't as familiar with the layout here as at Santa Theresita, but clubhouses were all pretty much the same—more betting windows, a bar and a sandwich stand, small tables facing a TV that broadcast the races being run.

The TV was dark now, but a couple of trainers Dan knew slightly were sitting at one of the tables. One of them, a burly redheaded man looked up. His eyes met Dan's, and he nodded. At least the man didn't give him the cold shoulder. He glanced at Cassie. "Do you mind if I leave you alone for a minute? There's someone over there I need to speak to."

"Sure." She smiled. "What kind of sandwich do you want?"

"Anything..."

She watched him walk over to the table. No one else would have noticed the tension in his carriage, but she knew Dan so well now, she could see it. Something to do with the mystery of why he'd left racetrack work? It had to be, she thought.

Dan's talk with the two men was brief—barely enough time for her to order and pay for sandwiches and drinks. As he turned back in her direction, the men he had spoken with rose and left the clubhouse. Cassie zeroed in on Dan's shoulders. A slump of defeat? Or was she only imagining things?

"Sorry to abandon you," he said lightly, but she could hear the strain he was trying to conceal from her.

"No problem." She handed him a cellophane-wrapped sandwich. Roast beef. She knew he liked roast beef. Then she said gently, "Don't you think you'd better tell me about it, Dan?"

He blinked, then said slowly, "I should have known you'd figure out that something was bothering me."

She nodded. "It's pretty obvious sometimes."

"Like just now, for instance." He shot a quick glance at the table the two men had vacated. "I have to warn you, Cassie. It's not a pretty story."

Was that why he hadn't told her before? she wondered. "That's okay. I think I can handle it."

He led her over to the table nearest the wall. They sat, and as Cassie unwrapped her sandwich, Dan said, "To begin, I have to fill in a little history." He told her how he had met Arthur Winwood, owner of the Willow Run training stables, when one of Winwood's horses was operated on at the specialized equine facility in Pennsylvania where Dan was completing his last year of residency.

Winwood and Dan had taken an immediate liking to each other. "Come on out to the West Coast when you're done here," Winwood had suggested. "We could use an up-to-date young fellow like you."

He had guaranteed Dan all the veterinary work for the sixty or so horses he trained. "I'll put a good word in for you with the other owners and trainers, too," Winwood had promised. "You ought to do just fine."

And so he had, for nearly five years. Like most track vets, he had worked for a number of different people. But Arthur Winwood, with his huge stable, had always been by far his most important client. That was fine, too, as far as Dan was concerned. He and the old man had seen eye-to-eye on the care of Thoroughbreds. For both of them, the health and safety of the animals came first.

Then Arthur Winwood had died, leaving Willow Run to his nephew Owen. The younger man had worked with his uncle for the previous couple of years, seeming to agree with his methods and practices, so even though Dan had grieved for Arthur, he had expected his job to continue much as before.

"But I was wrong," Dan said to Cassie, a bitter cast to his voice. "Two weeks after Owen Winwood took over, he entered a horse in a race, an animal I knew had been nerved up on the leg." He glanced at Cassie to see if she understood.

She nodded, knowing that it was a fairly common and safe practice to eliminate lameness by severing nerves low in an injured horse's heel. When it was necessary to perform a similar operation higher up, though, the animal lost all feeling in the leg. She could guess that racing a horse in that condition was bound to be extremely dangerous. Without sensation in the limb, the horse could trip and break a leg, perhaps injuring his jockey or other horses and riders.

"I knew the horse could break down if he ran," Dan said, "so I told Winwood I'd report him to the racing authorities if he insisted on entering the horse."

By now Cassie was on the edge of her chair. "What happened?"

"The horse didn't run." Dan paused. "Winwood fired me, of course."

Cassie's frown was sympathetic. "That must have been tough. But you did save the horse."

"Not for long. Winwood ran the horse the following week at another track. He broke down completely, fell, and had to be destroyed."

Dan had scarcely touched his sandwich. Now Cassie felt her own appetite deserting her. "That's terrible!" she exclaimed. "I can't believe anyone would do that to a horse."

Dan nodded. "Yes, it was terrible. It shouldn't have happened. Unfortunately I didn't hear about it until a few weeks later. By then, there was nothing I could do."

"Why not? You could still have reported Winwood to the authorities, couldn't you?"

Dan shook his head. "By then, my credibility had been destroyed." Either out of pure spite or in self-defense, Winwood had begun spreading stories about Dan. Along with general accusations of incompetence, he had intimated that Dan was guilty of injecting lame horses with synthetic morphine—not only an illegal practice, but a hot issue in the racing world. Tests to discover the presence of the synthetic were expensive and difficult, only done when there was a reason to suspect its use. The reputable owners and trainers Dan worked for shied like frightened colts from a vet supposed to be unprincipled enough to use the substance.

"Couldn't you have sued for slander?" Cassie asked.

"I thought about it," Dan said. "But it was all whispers and innuendos. When I confronted Winwood, he simply denied having said any such thing."

All the same, clients had quickly drifted away. No one said much to Dan about the rumors; he just didn't get called to treat injured or ill animals. When he went to the track, people had turned away with, at best, cursory greetings.

"It was partly my fault," Dan said. "Working as much as I did for Willow Run, I hadn't developed very strong relationships with other owners and trainers. They just didn't know me that well. If I hadn't always let Willow Run come first, I might have been in a better position to defend myself when this happened."

"You couldn't have known," Cassie said.

Whatever the reasons, within weeks Dan had found the doors to racing closed to him. Then he had noticed Doc Anderson's ad in a veterinary journal. "I needed something to do," Dan explained. "I was going crazy just sitting around all day. But at the same time, I knew it would be a mistake for me just to disappear. That's why I came to L.A., those other times. To let people at the races see I hadn't gone away because I was ashamed of anything."

"I understand," Cassie said. "I just wish you'd told me before." It would have saved her worrying and wondering about those trips he'd made. *Sure it would*, she thought ironically. It wouldn't have saved her any worry at all. Oh, she'd have understood the reason for his visits . . . and *known*, long before now, that he was searching for ways to leave Pinetop.

"I wanted to tell you," Dan said. More than once it had been on the tip of his tongue to explain what had happened. But he'd known intuitively that Cassie wouldn't want to hear that he was actively trying to get back to racing.

But that was another issue for another time. Not that it could be postponed much longer. If Doc Anderson sold his practice to Ohlson, it would be time for Dan to go. He couldn't just hang around Pinetop, waiting for something to change for him in racing. And when he did leave, he wanted Cassie to go with him. He knew it wouldn't be easy for her, uprooting herself from the town she loved, but surely she cared enough for him to do it. He *knew* she cared. He could see it at this very moment, in the sympathy in her eyes.

She leaned across the table and covered his hand with hers. "I'm so sorry, Dan." And she *was* sorry, sorry about the injustice done to him, the pain he'd felt and was still feeling. But she couldn't wholeheartedly regret that that same injustice had brought him to Pinetop and into her life.

"Thanks. I appreciate that," he said.

She swallowed. "And how is it now? Those men you were talking to . . ."

The bitterness in his voice returned. "Let's just say that they didn't especially welcome me with open arms." He exhaled a harsh breath. "I guess I've been a fool. I thought by now, people would have seen through Winwood, seen what kind of man he is."

"They will," she said loyally. And when they did, Dan's reputation would be cleansed . . . and she would lose him.

Dan turned his hand in hers and squeezed her fingers. "Cassie . . ." he said.

But before he could go on, a voice said, "Faraday!"

Cassie looked up. The man who had spoken was tall and expensively clothed, with a head of thick gray hair that was exquisitely cut and groomed. His smile was broad with ultrastraight, ultrawhite teeth. Expensive dental work, too, Cassie thought.

He extended his hand and Dan rose to shake it, then introduced him to Cassie as Douglas Pargeter.

"Somebody said they'd seen you here today," Pargeter said to Dan.

Dan repressed a grimace as he muttered something noncommittal. He could imagine what Pargeter had heard . . . probably from one of the trainers he'd spoken to earlier. Something about "the gall of that Faraday guy, showing up in the clubhouse, bold as brass, after what *he* did." He cautioned himself not to get paranoid. There was nothing but friendliness in Pargeter's manner.

Douglas Pargeter was the owner of a hugely successful breeding and training establishment a few hours north of

L.A. and one of the few breeders to employ his own full-time vet. Dan had never worked on any of Pargeter's horses, but it mattered a lot to Dan what Pargeter thought. The man had the reputation of being of the same stamp as Arthur Winwood—upright, inflexibly honest, always putting the well-being of the horses above any other consideration. Now that Arthur was gone, Doug Pargeter was probably the man Dan respected most in West Coast racing.

Dan said, as he'd said to others during his previous visits to the track, "There's one thing I'd like to get on the record, Pargeter. I didn't do the things Owen Winwood accused me of."

Others he had said this to had turned away, often in disgust, as if Dan's statement of his innocence had been in bad taste. But Pargeter met his eye directly. "I never thought you did."

Relief drove the air from Dan's lungs. At least one person—and an important person, at that—believed in his integrity. "Thanks," he said. "That's good to hear." A *slight* understatement. It was the first real breach he'd discovered in the wall Owen Winwood had built, the wall that had shut Dan out of racing. He gestured at the empty chair pulled up to their table. "Would you care to join us?"

Pargeter hesitated for only an instant. "Let me get myself a beer first. I'll be right back."

Dan sat down as Pargeter walked away. Cassie glanced at him and said in an undertone, "He's important, isn't he?"

Dan nodded, no longer surprised by the acuity of her perceptions. He had learned over the past weeks that she picked up on things many people would have missed.

In a moment Pargeter returned, carrying a paper cupful of beer. At first it was all small talk. Pargeter asked Dan where he'd been and what he'd been doing, and Dan explained that he'd been filling in for another man's practice.

Soon the conversation turned to horses, Pargeter mentioning the ones he had running that day and dispassionately discussing each one's chances. But then he gave Dan a long level look. "I take it from what you've said, Faraday, that this job you're doing now is only temporary. Does that mean you haven't necessarily left racing for good?"

Cassie stared numbly at her hands. She already knew what he would say. If he didn't want to return to racing, he wouldn't be here, wouldn't have made those other visits to the track.

Dan shrugged. "That depends, I guess, on whether there's any work available to me."

In reply, Pargeter said only, "Hmm."

Cassie shot the man a swift glance. There was something in his tone that had invested a normally noncommittal noise with great significance.

Dan heard the "Hmm," too, and wondered. The vet Pargeter employed was getting along in years, nearing retirement age. Was there a chance, even a remote one, that Pargeter was starting to look around for a replacement? If so, and if Pargeter was considering him for the job, it would be the perfect solution to *all* his problems. A vet who worked for Pargeter would live near the man's farm. It wouldn't be the city—the high-rises, the traffic, the smog—that Cassie hated.

Things that sounded too good to be true often were just that, Dan reminded himself. He was probably leaping to a whole bunch of hasty conclusions. If he was smart, he wouldn't even dare to hope.

Soon after, Pargeter rose. "I'd better get going. I've got a filly running in the second race." He paused and said to Dan, "That town you're working in is called Pinetop, you said?"

Dan nodded.

"Information would have your phone number? I might want to chat about this and that sometime."

Again, Dan nodded. He felt a nerve pulsing in his jaw. Another reason to hope? He doubted if Pargeter was the type to want to "chat" without a purpose. "Call me anytime," he said, trying to sound casual.

Pargeter said goodbye and took one step away from the table. But then he turned back. "Oh, one more thing..." He lowered his voice. "I probably shouldn't say anything at this stage, but I figure you deserve to hear it. A little bird tells me that the HBPA's looking into some of Owen Winwood's practices." He nodded once, brusquely. Then he was gone.

A slow smile curved Dan's lips. "Well, I'll be damned!"

"What is it, Dan?" Cassie asked. "What's the HBPA?"

"The Horseman's Benevolent Protective Association. The governing body of racing. They have their own investigators...and they're good!" His grin stretched his mouth wide. "Looks like that bastard's going to get what he deserves."

And exonerate Dan in the process? Cassie wondered. Almost certainly. And then what?

And then he would leave her, she thought miserably. But she couldn't let her face show how she felt when Dan was so happy. She said enthusiastically, "That's terrific!"

"Yes, it is, isn't it?" He took her hand and pulled her to her feet. "Come on, honey. Let's go bet on a horse. I feel lucky today."

CASSIE YAWNED and snuggled against Dan's side as they walked from his van to the back door of her house. By dint of great effort, she had managed to cast aside her worries about the future in order to concentrate on the present. Pretty successful, she had been, too, once she'd put her mind to it. "What a wonderful day! Thank you, Dan."

"I had a great time, too."

She pushed open the back door to be met by Blunder, who wriggled as if she'd been gone for weeks instead of having left only that morning. It felt like more than a day to Cassie, too. First there'd been the races, where she had made a whopping four-dollar profit on her minimal bets. Then came dinner at a charming place downtown that she had heard about while living in L.A., but never had been able to afford. It was called The Pacific Dining Car, and one of the sections was an actual train car. The food had been delicious. And then the show . . .

She sighed rapturously. "The songs! The dancing! It was all just great."

Dan helped her off with her coat and draped it over a kitchen chair, then he circled her waist with his arms. He couldn't resist needling her, just a little. "You liked the show, I gather."

"I loved it."

"You mean you're admitting that *some* good things happen in a big city?" He didn't want to confess that, after little more than six weeks away from L.A., he had found the crowds and the struggle for a parking space a bit wearing.

He was unprepared for how serious Cassie's face became in response to his casual jibe. "I never said there was *nothing* good about city life," she said. "I can't deny that you don't get entertainment or restaurants like that up here. But just look at the plus side."

"Hey!" Dan protested. "I didn't mean this to turn into a full-scale debate."

She looped her hands around his neck, but her expression didn't lighten. "You started it."

He sighed. This was going to get more serious than he wanted to be tonight. Unless he deflected her somehow . . . And he knew exactly the method to use. "Okay. Tell me about the plus side."

"Knowing your neighbors and being able to count on them, that's number one," she said promptly, then let out a little squeak. "Dan, what are you doing?"

"Kissing your neck. You have a delicious neck. Have I ever told you that?" His mouth nibbled up the side of her throat. "What else?"

"What else what? Oh, you mean about Pinetop?"

"Mmm-hmm."

He took her earlobe between his lips, then probed the interior of her ear with the tip of his tongue. His hands had gotten into the act, too. They were on her front, his knuckles grazing the underside of her breasts.

Cassie squirmed. "Then there's the space and the air."

"And the snow and the sleet," Dan countered.

"And the changing of the seasons. You don't get that in—" She broke off as Dan shifted tactics. His mouth was at her temples, but his hands had moved up on her breasts, and his thumbs rubbed back and forth over her hardening nipples.

"You don't get what in what?" he prompted.

"What?" She was breathing heavily. Even at two in the morning and worn out, desire for Dan sprang readily into life. The heat of it was building in her lower body; her skin felt ultrasensitized to his touch.

"Running out of arguments?" he teased.

"Of course not. I was trying to say that you don't get . . ."

Without ceasing the maddeningly pleasurable friction on her breasts, Dan moved his lower body against hers. She could feel his erection rising beneath his trousers.

"Oh, shoot! I don't know," she said. "Let's go to bed."

"Wise woman," Dan said approvingly. "Bed it is." He turned her in the direction of her bedroom. But then, abruptly, he stopped. When Cassie glanced up at him to in-

quire the reason, she saw he had a wicked twinkle in his eyes.
"I just had a better idea," he said. "Let's *not* go to bed."

"What?" She frowned. "You mean stay up all night?"

"No, that's not what I mean." He leaned over and whispered in her ear.

Cassie giggled. "I don't know. I can foresee all kinds of problems. But I guess it's worth a try."

"I WARNED YOU the hay would be prickly," Cassie said some time later. Dan had suggested that they needn't wait for spring after all, to try making love in the barn. The electric heater she'd put in the tack room for Willie was now in the one empty stall, and Dan was sitting in the middle of the deceptively soft-looking pile of hay, stripped to shorts and shirt and shifting uncomfortably.

"No, you didn't," he said indignantly. "You didn't say a thing about it."

"Well, I thought it," she countered.

"Oh ho, so the lady expects me to read her mind!"

"You do sometimes," she said.

"Yeah . . ." A slow smile curved his mouth. "Sometimes, I do. And sometimes, you read mine." He scrunched up his face in a parody of intense thought. "Try reading it right now!"

"You're trying to figure out how we're going to manage this project of ours without getting poked in uncomfortable places by pieces of hay," she said.

"You got it!" He paused. "Hmm. Don't I remember seeing some blankets in the tack room?"

"You do, indeed." She turned toward the door of the stall, but Dan stopped her. Springing up from his reclining position, he said, "I'll go get a couple. You assume the appropriate attire."

"Which is?"

"Skin. Nothing but skin." Glorious, beautiful skin. The glow she got after they'd made love was something he never tired of seeing. Knowing he could bring that flush to her cheeks and throat, apparently any time at all, was the most erotic thing he'd ever experienced. All he had to do was picture her response to find himself . . . feeling as he felt now. Aching for her, and with a bulge in his jockey shorts to prove it.

He made a mad dash down the aisle to the tack room. As he went, a horse whickered from its stall. Commenting to his fellows on the oddity of these humans, Dan fancied.

Returning with the two softest blankets over his arm, he looked over the stall half door. The sight that greeted him brought a lump to his throat. Cassie was undressed, lying in the hay, arms extended toward him.

What he felt, looking at her, was too important for words to express. There would be no games tonight, despite the unusualness of their surroundings. The tenderness he felt, the love, was too big for play. He went in and knelt beside her and tried to make his embrace tell her how he felt.

The moment Dan touched her, Cassie knew that this was not going to be a time for lightheartedness, and she was relieved. Deep down, beneath her surface enjoyment of the day they'd spent, was a heavy layer of sorrow. She'd gotten a partial answer to the question she hadn't wanted to ask; Dan would leave Pinetop if he could. It was only a matter of time until his reputation was restored. The HBPA's investigation into Owen Winwood virtually guaranteed it now. And there was Pargeter's meaningful "Hmm" to factor into the equation.

So now she knew. The only remaining uncertainty was when, how long. And her only possible out was the faint possibility that Dan would change his mind and decide to

stay, after all. Only a fool would cling to that one, she told
herself.

Instead, she clung to Dan, holding him tight, then turning
her head to invite his kiss. His lips were soft. So soft at first.
Then harder, more demanding. She somehow finished re-
moving his clothes, while he went on kissing her, though she
couldn't remember actually doing it.

And Dan somehow managed, still kissing her, to spread
the blankets over the pile of hay. They sank into the soft
mound together. His legs twined with hers, and he began caressing her. Slowly. Gently. The languorous sensations that
invaded Cassie's body made it easy for her to match his
rhythm with her own caresses on his back, his thighs, his firm
belly. She sighed with pleasure and Dan's sigh answered hers.

It might have been moments or hours later when he entered her. Not a thrust, but a slow easing of himself into her
waiting warmth. She had never felt more attuned with him,
more as if his body and hers were truly one. For a long time,
he remained motionless inside her, still caressing her with his
hands. Only when her internal muscles involuntarily tensed
around him did he begin to move. It was all slow motion, an
exquisite pas de deux between two partners who knew each
other's movements intimately. And though the sensations
were exquisite, Cassie began to fear that for once, out of all
the times they had made love, this time she wouldn't achieve
release. Not that it mattered, she told herself. The experience alone was lovely.

But then, without his tempo quickening, she began to
move, responding to a profound need deep within her. Her
hips arched and twisted, lifting and turning in rhythm with
Dan. And the slow waves of pleasure that finally rippled
through her were in tempo, too, and she softened in a release
that was no less complete than the cataclysm that sometimes
overtook her.

A sigh came from deep in Dan's chest as his final strokes took him to the same quiet resolution. He eased himself down on her, the hay beneath them helping to absorb his weight. He was still inside her, her arms locked around his back, when Cassie's eyelids drifted shut.

She woke up only a little as he carried her to the house. "The heater..." she murmured drowsily.

"It's unplugged. I put it back in the tack room."

She managed to summon enough energy to lift her hand and caress the back of his head. "The way we made love out there, Dan... It was..."

"I know, sweetheart," he said, and kissed her on the cheek.

12

A WEEK PASSED. A new Monday came around and with it Kevin Ohlson, the vet who was interested in buying the practice. Dan came out of his office into the reception area to find Ohlson grilling Ellen on the rates for various services. One look at the man's pointed, weasely face, and it was hate at first sight—a feeling which only intensified when Ohlson sat down across from Dan in the office and said, "I suppose you realize this place is a potential gold mine, Faraday."

"It is?" Although a vet could make a comfortable living here, Dan couldn't imagine anyone getting rich off Pinetop's assorted animals.

"Sure. The only vet in town! The trick is to hike the prices gradually. A few people might take their pets somewhere else for the routine stuff, but it's a helluva drive down that mountain. And in an emergency, they'd have to come here."

"Isn't that unethical?" Dan suggested, trying to keep a grip on himself when what he really wanted to do was lunge across the desk and rip Ohlson's face off.

Ohlson snickered. "It's a dog-eat-dog world out there, Faraday. You got to make it how you can."

Dan wasted no time after Ohlson's departure in getting on the phone to Doc Anderson. The older man listened as Dan gave an account of Ohlson's visit, then said, shocking Dan, "Well, so be it. I never thought I could legislate the morals of my successor."

"But you've said how important it is to you to get the right man," Dan protested.

"The right man doesn't want it. Unless you've changed your mind...."

He had the feeling Doc Anderson was trying to manipulate him into buying the practice, even using the loathsome Ohlson as a lever. But he wouldn't be manipulated. That would be to give up any hope of ever returning to the track. He said nothing.

Doc Anderson went on, with a trace of reluctance in his voice, "I also don't want this thing hanging on forever. I'll try to stall Ohlson for a while and hope someone else turns up, but, candidly, the offer he's made is very generous."

Dan hung up, seething at the thought of a slime like Kevin Ohlson sitting at *his* desk, dealing with *his* patients. Only they weren't his, he reminded himself. He was a racehorse vet and working with racehorses was where he belonged.

He wouldn't even be able to relieve his feelings by telling Cassie about Ohlson, he thought regretfully. It was too closely related to the question of his leaving Pinetop, and he didn't want to upset her when the situation was still so vague. Until he had lined up work elsewhere or until Doc Anderson actually agreed to sell the practice, Dan couldn't be sure what his options were. So there was no point in discussing what he hoped would be Cassie's place in his future.

Feeling a new urgency, he stayed in his office during lunch hour and typed a couple of letters, feelers for racetrack work. With the letters addressed and stamped, he took a folder from his desk drawer. The town meeting was tonight, and he was presenting the report for the committee that had investigated the Partyland project. He spent the rest of his lunch hour reviewing his notes and had just put them away, readying himself for his first patient of the afternoon, when the phone buzzed.

He picked it up and Ellen said, "A Mr. Douglas Pargeter for you on line two, Doc."

"Thanks, Ellen." He noticed an actual tremor in his hand as he reached for the button on the phone and switched to the outside line.

Ten minutes later, Dan hung up the phone, smiling. It wasn't definite, but it sounded as if . . .

Ellen tapped on the office door. "You've got a patient waiting in the treatment room, Doc."

"Sorry, Ellen. I know I'm running a little late." He paused. "I hate to ask you to do this, but I have to go down the mountain on Wednesday. I'll be gone the whole day. Will you reschedule my appointments?"

"Sure, Doc." Ellen hesitated in the doorway.

"Something else?"

Her lips thinned to a narrow line. "I just wanted to tell you that if that creep who was here this morning buys the practice, I'm quitting."

"It hasn't happened yet."

"But if it does . . ." Ellen shook her head. "Doc, it's none of my business, but you've settled in here so well . . . Couldn't you . . . ?"

"No, Ellen. I'm afraid not," he said firmly.

"SUMMING UP, the committee feels that Pinetop should okay Partyland's request for a zoning variance." Dan looked out at the faces of his friends and neighbors. Once he hit his stride, the report had gone just fine, but he had been surprised at how nervous he'd been when he began. It was because these people had placed their trust in him, and he hadn't wanted to let them down.

He looked toward Cassie, who was seated with Jack and Mary Jo near the middle of the meeting hall, and was rewarded by her smile.

Cassie herself felt like a proud mother whose child had acquitted himself honorably at the school pageant. Only there was a flaw in the analogy, she realized at once. There was absolutely nothing motherly about her feelings for Dan. He was all man—with none of the need for pampering and babying that some little-boy men never outgrew.

There were questions from the floor, which Dan and the other committee members fielded. No, the people in Bear Valley had no complaints about the Partyland facility there. It had provided work for the teens of the community and that was a big plus.

Before the vote was taken, the mayor, Calvin Engalls, asked for a hand for the folks on the committee, and Pinetop responded with a hearty round of applause. Mary Jo murmured in Cassie's ear, "They really did a good job on this, didn't they? They must have put in a lot of time."

"They did," Cassie said. Dan and the other committee members had made several trips to Bear Valley. And there had been two long meetings with Partyland representatives sent to Pinetop for that purpose. Seeing the extent to which Dan had thrown himself into the project had encouraged Cassie's inclination to hope. Day by day, since their visit to the track, she had found herself building an edifice of optimism, and she added to the walls of hope any little sign of his integration into Pinetop life. Yet she knew what a shaky construction it really was. Offered work in racing, Dan would be off like a shot.

Pargeter's "Hmm" kept echoing in her ears. If she were a better person, she had told herself repeatedly, she would hope that Pargeter would offer Dan a job, since that was what he wanted. She wanted Dan to be happy, but she wanted him to be happy here, with her. Which just went to show what a rotten, despicable character she really was.

The mayor called for the vote on the zoning issue then announced in his best pontifical style, "The will of the town being overwhelmingly in favor of the zoning variance, it is so ordered." He banged his gavel down.

Several people rose, assuming this signaled the end of the meeting. But the mayor said loudly, "Now, wait just a minute, folks! We're not done yet."

With a few grumbles, those who had risen took their seats. Mayor Engalls said, "Now, it seems to me that we'll need another committee to kinda keep tabs on this Partyland project as it goes along." Seeming to realize that he had lapsed too far into informality, he cleared his throat. "Naturally, I'll be monitoring it myself, to ascertain that the agreement between the corporation and the township is being carried out in all particulars."

"Can it, Mr. Mayor," said someone from the floor. "Get to the point!"

"Yes, the point," said the mayor, looking slightly flustered. "The point, ah . . ."

"A new committee," Fred Willard prompted helpfully.

"Yes, exactly." Mayor Engalls turned toward Dan, who still stood near the podium. "May I assume that you'd be willing to serve, Doctor Faraday? It would be ideal if you would. To keep the continuity going and ensure that . . ."

Cassie failed to hear the rest of what the Mayor said. Her focus was on Dan, standing tall and handsome at the front of the room . . . and shaking his head no.

Her stomach lurched. No, because he wouldn't be around to fulfill the committee's task? Or no because he felt he'd done enough?

When the mayor had finally wound down, Dan said, "Thank you, Mr. Mayor, but I'm afraid I must decline."

Mary Jo leaned sideways and whispered in Cassie's ear, "How come he's not accepting?"

Cassie bit her lip. "I don't know. I . . ." She mustered up all her essential optimism. But it was more difficult than usual. "Maybe he feels he's done enough already," she said.

Mary Jo looked skeptical, but said nothing more.

The mayor went on to appoint a committee, then finally banged his gavel for the last time. "Meeting adjourned."

Cassie stood and looked toward the front of the room. The mayor seemed to be making a speech to Dan and the other committee members. As she moved into the aisle, she heard Marj Simmons's voice a row or two back, speaking a familiar name. She turned and saw the town historian talking with Sandra Maxwell.

She joined the two women. It was easier to worry about this than to worry about what Dan's declining of the committee post did or didn't mean. "Did I hear you say something about Willie Wilson?" she asked Marj. She had wondered about Willie during the past couple of weeks, but she hadn't seen him anywhere.

Marj said, "I was just telling Sandra that the sheriff caught Willie sleeping in some summer people's cabin. He must have been staying there for quite a while, the sheriff said."

Cassie inhaled sharply. "What did the sheriff do with Willie?"

Marj shrugged. "There was no damage done and nothing taken, so Sheriff Johnson just locked him up overnight. Then this morning he told Willie to get out of town." She leaned closer to Cassie. "Between you and me, I have a hunch the sheriff slipped Willie a few bucks before he sent him on his way."

Sheriff Johnson was on the other side of the room. The middle-aged man affected a hard-as-nails exterior, but everyone in town knew, without letting on to the sheriff, that inside he was soft as a marshmallow.

"I wonder where Willie went," Cassie mused aloud.

"I imagine, with a few bucks in his jeans to tide him over, he would have hitched a ride back down the mountain," Marj suggested.

"I bet you're right." Cassie felt a measure of relief. At the back of her mind, she was sorting out what she would say to Dan when he joined her. Ask him why he'd refused to serve on the committee? Of course, he had every right to decline. It didn't have to mean anything.

But at least she didn't have to fret over Willie anymore. When he was still in Pinetop, she often wondered where he spent his nights. Knowing he was in a climate where he wouldn't freeze if he had to sleep outdoors was a much less worrying thought.

She looked around for Jack and Mary Jo, wondering if they'd like to join Dan and her for a beer at the Pizza Bar, but they had gone. She had noticed that the pair had seemed awkward with each other tonight. Not surprising, Cassie thought. Poor Jack was still waiting for Mary Jo to make up her mind. Poor Mary Jo was still torn by indecision.

Dan had finally escaped from the mayor, Cassie saw, but even so, his progress toward her was slow. Every few feet someone stopped him to thank him for his efforts on the town's behalf or to congratulate him on the excellence of his report.

He finally reached her. In the foyer they put on coats and scarves, then went outside. A freezing rain had fallen most of the day, and the steps were shiny with ice. As Dan took Cassie's arm, Clem Jones brushed past them. "Great job, Doc. Sure wish you'da been on that new committee, though, to keep an eye on things."

Cassie shot Dan a swift sideways glance as Clem went on down the steps. "That committee you were on *was* a lot of work," she said. "I don't blame you a bit for not wanting to get involved in a whole lot more."

Dan said nothing. He had intended to tell her right after the meeting about Pargeter's call. It was one of his reasons, though not his only one, for refusing to serve on the committee. Pargeter or no Pargeter, he wouldn't have been in Pinetop long enough to see the job through. But he decided to postpone the conversation a little longer. Tonight in her bed, holding her in his arms, would be the best place for all the things he had to say.

SNUG IN CASSIE'S BED, Dan pulled the covers over both their heads, making a warm and secret place for their lovemaking.

She drew her fingertips down his bare chest, savoring the combination of crisp hair and smooth skin. "The only trouble with this," she complained lightly, "is that it's too dark under here. I can't *see* you."

"That is a problem." Dan's warm breath fanned her cheek, setting loose a quiver of anticipation in her belly. "I guess we'll just have to do as the blind do."

"Braille lovemaking?" Cassie shot back.

"Clever girl."

She felt him bend and move, felt the pull of the sheet and blankets that covered them, but she had no idea where he was heading. It was a shock—though a pleasant one—when his lips touched her toes. He kissed all ten, but the littlest ones he sucked in his mouth and the quivers in Cassie's stomach moved lower and turned into throbs of pleasure.

"I had no idea," she murmured.

Dan's voice came from the bottom of the bed. "No idea about what?"

"That toes could be . . ." A gasp interrupted her sentence; Dan's hand had moved up her leg to the back of her knee. Normally she was ticklish there. Not now. His fingers moving on the soft crease made her squirm with delight. As always Dan's lovemaking erased all her fears and concerns. Later, thoughts of him declining to be on the committee, and

Pargeter's "Hmm" would return, but for now, she could revel in what his body did to hers.

She inhaled, then managed to say, "No idea that toes could be an erogenous zone."

Already she was behind the times, she discovered. His tongue was on the arch of her foot—another unsuspected source of erotic pleasure.

Her eyes were adjusting somewhat to the darkness. She could make out the shape of Dan's body. By curving her own torso, she was able to reach his flat belly. She had learned sometime back that he liked to be caressed there. She trailed her fingertips from hip bone to hip bone and back again. His breathing, like hers, grew more labored, but he continued to move smoothly up her body. His hands were on her thighs, his mouth at her knee.

Cassie moved her hand and brushed the tip of his erection. His groan, as he planted a hot wet kiss on her inner thigh, made her thrill with the knowledge of how deeply she could pleasure him. She circled the hard smooth length of him with her fingers and rubbed the way she knew he liked her to.

"Whoa! Slow down, Cassie. I want—" He expelled a sharp gust of breath before he could go on. "I want to do some more exploring first."

Cassie stopped moving her hand, but left her fingers wrapped around him. His heat seemed to permeate her skin and spread throughout her entire body, centering low down and becoming a steady ache of desire. "It doesn't seem fair," she said breathlessly. "You're doing all the work."

"My turn to be the love slave," he said. "You don't *always* get to have all the fun, you know."

She smiled. With a soft sigh, she lay back. As Dan's hands and mouth performed their magic, she grew pliant, as if her bones were gradually liquifying. He kissed her everywhere, even turning her onto her side, so he could tongue the small of her back while his hands caressed her buttocks.

By the time he returned her to her original position, her need was a throbbing, ecstatic torment. Her head moved back and forth, her breath coming in short gasping pants. Her knees opened wide, and she reached for Dan to guide him into her.

But he gently took her hand away and slid lower on her body to bestow burning kisses on her inner thighs. He dipped a finger into an intimate fold, then followed the finger's path with his mouth. His tongue flicked across her swollen bud, propelling her into a shattering climax.

He held her, muttering love sounds as her shuddering died away. And then, when she thought he would surely enter her, he began again—caressing, kissing, until she was hurled over another brink of sensation into another sweet release.

Only then did he poise himself over her. It was not because of lack of desire that he had held back so long. Cassie, touching his upper body as he lowered himself onto her, could feel his passion in the fine tremor of his muscles, the corded tendons of his neck.

As he sheathed himself in her, he gave a low moan of satisfaction. His swift deep strokes brought Cassie a new rush of sensation. She arched upward, wrapping her legs around him, drawing him more deeply within her. The shuddering of his body as he climaxed pushed Cassie's own excitement to the limits. Her legs tight around him, she held him inside her as she experienced yet another paroxysm of pleasure and release.

They held each other in satiated silence for a long time before Dan flipped the covers away from their heads. The bed was a wreck, sheets and blankets pulled out and twisted. Cassie slipped out of bed to straighten the covers. She hated being away from Dan's warm body, and she hurried as fast as she could.

When she climbed back into bed, he put his arm around her. Nestled against his side, she said succinctly, "Wow!"

"Not a bad choice of words," he said with a grin. "Wow, indeed!" But then, he sobered. His dark eyes were grave. "I don't know if I've ever told you properly how lovely you are, Cassie."

She murmured a demurral—she thought he'd done just fine at telling her, many times—but he said, "You're lovely here." He cupped a hand over her feminine mound, then smoothed his hand up her belly to her breast. "And lovely here." Then he touched the place between her breasts, the place emblematic of her heart. "And especially here." He kissed her temples. "And here."

A warm glow surrounded Cassie. That he was lavish with loving words and gestures when no longer in the grip of passion was especially meaningful to her. "You're okay yourself, Doc," she said lightly, then tried to say with a hug followed by gentle caresses what she felt she was not eloquent enough to put into words. She touched his shoulder, ruffled his hair, planted a kiss on his chest. "And you really did a terrific job on that report."

His eyebrows lifted. "Just on the report?" he teased.

"Let's just say that you're a man of many talents."

He smiled, then eased slightly away from her, scooting up against the headboard. "I aim to please," he said, then went on without a change in his tone. "I have something to tell you, Cassie. Douglas Pargeter called me this afternoon . . . about a job."

One subject to another, without warning. Her heart flipped over, and she sat up against the headboard for support.

For a moment she suspected Dan of having made a special effort to give her pleasure tonight in order to soften her up for this conversation. But almost at once she knew that was wrong, that she was being unfair to accuse him. He always made a special effort, and her pleasure in their lovemaking was always intense.

Pride made her try to conceal how devastated she felt. "Oh? You must be very happy about it."

"Cassie..." Dan frowned. This wasn't the reaction he'd expected. It took him only an instant to see through her pretense. He put his arms around her and tried to pull her unyielding body closer to his. It was like embracing a stone. "Listen, honey," he said, "I know what you're thinking."

"I doubt it." Her voice was cool, but a little tremor in it gave her away.

"Well, maybe not exactly, but I bet I can come pretty close. You're thinking this is more or less good-bye."

"Isn't it?"

"No. The job isn't definite, but even if it were..." He struggled to find the right words and decided to start again, from a different angle. "I'm going down the mountain day after tomorrow to look the place over and talk to Pargeter. I'd like you to go with me."

Cassie shook her head no. Why should she visit the place that was going to take Dan away from her?

Dan drew a deep breath. He knew how she felt about Pinetop, but he also knew she cared about him as deeply as he cared for her. There was no other answer she could give but yes. "If I take this job, I'd like you to come with me, live with me. Don't say anything, Cassie. Not yet. It's not L.A. It's a rural area. The nearest town—Solvang—is small. Not as small as Pinetop, of course, but it's a far cry from a big city."

"You're asking me to go with you? Live with you?" He had mentioned something of the sort before, she remembered, during that talk they'd had out on the mountain, the day of their first ride together. But they hadn't even been lovers then, and she had more or less dismissed his tentative suggestion concerning a theoretical future.

"That's what I said." He frowned. "I don't know why you're acting so surprised. You must have thought about it."

She gave a swift shake of her head. If she *had* thought about it, she would have assumed Dan knew Pinetop was her home—that she couldn't just up and leave. They had talked a lot about so many different things. But apparently they hadn't talked enough...or not honestly enough. If they had, she thought, he would *know*. He wouldn't be suggesting the impossible.

Dan said slowly, "Actually, I was thinking that we might as well get married. Or we could wait a while. Whichever makes you feel more comfortable." He had thought a lot about this. He knew he was asking her to take a big step, a move that would disrupt her life. Eventually he wanted marriage, kids, the whole enchilada. But for now he would be content just to have her with him.

She said, "Married?"

"Sure. Why not?"

Cassie's mind was working slowly, as if it was freezing, shutting down. She seized on the first thought that worked its way to the surface. "For one thing, you've never said you loved me."

Dan reared back in astonishment, lightly bumping the back of his head against the headboard. He rubbed it regretfully. "Sure I have. Dozens of times."

"You've said you were *in* love with me. There's a difference. *In* love is a state that could be temporary. Love is...well, you know. Forever."

He let out a burst of delighted laughter. It was all right. Clear up this one little point, and she would be his. "Cassie McLean, I never would have thought you were the type to quibble over semantics. Okay. I'm *in* love with you, it's true. Definitely in a state over you. But I love you, too." Suddenly, he frowned. "I just realized. You've never said it, either." She'd always used the phrase "in love," just as he had.

"Oh, I love you, Dan. Definitely."

Her words were right, but the tone was all wrong, leaden enough that it damped his euphoria. He said determinedly, "Then you'll go with me? Assuming I get the job, of course."

"No."

That one little word dropped like a fifty-pound weight onto Dan's heart. She was still close against his side, but her warmth on his skin did nothing to ease the chill forming inside him.

She let out a long, painful-sounding sigh. "I'm glad to know you love me, too. I'm flattered that you would want to marry me. But I've made no secret about how I feel about living here in Pinetop."

"Cassie . . ." She moved away from him. Even the surface contact of skin against skin was lost to him. And he was only just beginning to realize how large the gap was between their minds.

"Even if I wanted to leave," she went on, "which I don't, how could I? There's the stable, the horses."

"You could sell the stable. And the horses. Of course, you won't want to sell Kettle, but you wouldn't have to. You can keep horses in Solvang. Or wherever we decide to live."

She gave a swift blind shake of her head. "It's not just that. Pinetop's my life."

"More than I am, you mean," he said coldly. It was beginning to sink in. He had asked her to make a choice, and she had chosen against him. Obviously *love* didn't mean the same thing to her as it did to him. A life together. Raising kids. Growing old together.

In a flurry of bedsheets, she pulled her legs up under her and sat cross-legged, facing him. "What if I went with you, and it didn't work out? If I sold the stable, I'd have nothing to come back to, nowhere to go."

"Then don't sell the stable. Get someone to run it. I don't care."

"You just don't understand."

He drew his shoulders up. A little voice in the back of his mind told him he should have been prepared for this. She'd said over and over again how she felt about Pinetop. Not just in words. He'd seen it in her actions and her attitudes. But that voice was drowned out by anger. "Oh, I understand all right," he said bitterly. "I understand that the goddamn town means more to you than I do. You say you love me, but you don't care enough to compromise."

Stung by his anger, Cassie retorted, "I didn't hear *you* making any offers to compromise."

"Oh, really? I didn't ask you to move into a high-rise condo in L.A., did I? We'd be living in a place not all that much bigger than Pinetop. If that's not a compromise, what is?"

"That's where the job is," she pointed out. "If it *had* been in L.A., that's where you would have asked me to go."

"But it's not in L.A. The point is . . ." Fury and the knowledge of what he had to lose—had already lost—was muddling up his thinking. "I don't know what the hell the point is." He struggled to get a grip on himself. "Yes, I do," he said firmly. "Will you go with me when I visit Pargeter's place?"

"I already said no."

"I know you did. This is for the record. And you won't even consider leaving Pinetop with me when I go?" The worst of his anger had burned out fast; his voice was the colorless gray of the ashes inside him.

"I can't," she said piteously.

"You won't. There's a difference." Dan swung his legs out of bed, then picked up his jeans from the floor where he'd dropped them.

"You're leaving?"

"Right." He stuck his legs into his jeans and pulled up the zipper as if he wanted to punish something, and the zipper was handy. "Frankly, Cassie, it'd just be too painful waking up beside you in the morning." Assuming he got any sleep, which he doubted, no matter where he spent the night.

There was nothing she could say. It had all been said. She didn't watch him finish dressing. She couldn't bear to even glance at him as he left the room. But she heard his footsteps moving through the house. And she heard the back door close—not a slam, but a heartbreakingly final thud.

She wouldn't cry, she told herself. She had no right to cry. From the very beginning with Dan, she'd known that it would come to this. Never mind that she'd temporarily deluded herself into thinking it might be different. At the very least, she could take her lumps dry-eyed.

She might have managed it if Blunder hadn't come through the bedroom door, which Dan had left open. Seeing Cassie huddled on the bed, her arms wrapped around herself, the dog whimpered and trotted over to her.

The touch of his cold nose on her bare leg acted as a trigger. Tears welled in her eyes; sobs erupted from her throat. Over and over, she kept saying to the anxious dog, "It's all right, Blunder. Don't worry. It's okay," as she cried and cried.

13

CASSIE SAT IN HER KITCHEN with a cup of cooling coffee on the table in front of her. It was Wednesday. A day and a night had passed since Dan left her bed. She hadn't seen him since, but she knew that by now he must be at Pargeter's place.

She stared dully at the pattern on the kitchen wallpaper. The funny thing about grief—which was essentially what she was experiencing, she had decided—was that it made her feel so tired. It had taken all her energy just to feed the horses this morning. Now, with a slight break in the weather to make it possible, she absolutely had to start exercising the animals, and she wasn't sure she was up to it.

She snorted contemptuously at herself. Not up to it, indeed! Anyone would think she was a pallid Victorian miss, pining away over a lost lover. Ridiculous!

A knock sounded on the back door. A reprieve, she thought. Whoever it was would give her a few minute's postponement before she had to drag herself out to perform a dreary round of activity that had never seemed the slightest bit dreary before.

She was surprised when she opened the door to see that her visitor was Mary Jo. Mary Jo, who ought to be at work right now. There were dark circles under the blonde's eyes, as if she hadn't been sleeping much. The two of them could form an insomniacs club, Cassie thought.

Forcing cheerfulness into her tone, she said, "Hi! This is a pleasant surprise. Playing hooky from your job?"

"Not exactly. I quit this morning."

"What?" Had Mary Jo lost her mind? Cassie wondered. Jobs in Pinetop were hard to come by.

"That's why I came to see you." Mary Jo pulled off her coat and sank onto a kitchen chair. "Pour me some of that coffee, will you? I have a lot to tell you."

Ten minutes later, Cassie was still shaking her head in disbelief. "But Chicago! Why on earth Chicago?" It was almost incidental, though saddening, that Mary Jo had turned down Jack's proposal of marriage and had broken off their relationship.

"Because that's where my uncle's brother-in-law's computer programming school is," Mary Jo said. "He's stretching a point and letting me have the family discount."

"I had no idea you were interested in computers."

"I don't know if I am or not. What I am interested in is developing some skill that'll get me a good job. A city job." She added grimly, "I'll learn to *love* computers, if that's what it takes."

"But Chicago is so far away."

Mary Jo nodded. "That's the other reason I'm going there. I thought about L.A., but it's too close. Jack could visit me there, or I could run up the mountain. A clean break'll be better for both of us. For Jack, too. Not just for me."

She was probably right. Mary Jo had been around Jack's entire life. Without her presence to keep his feelings for her alive, he might be able to find happiness with someone else. Sandra Maxwell, for instance. She'd always been fond of Jack. Maybe more than fond, Cassie thought, remembering the look she'd seen in Sandra's eyes once or twice, when Jack and Mary Jo were together.

But Mary Jo didn't look very happy about it at all. "Are you sure you're doing the right thing?"

"No," Mary Jo blurted. Then, after a moment's silence, she said, "Yes. I am sure. Jack and me—the things we want are just too different."

Tell me about it, Cassie thought ironically.

Mary Jo pulled herself up in her chair. "Let's discuss something more pleasant. How's it going with you and Dan?"

"More pleasant, hah!" said Cassie.

ABOUT THE TIME Cassie and Mary Jo were hugging each other and promising to write and call often, Dan was completing his tour of Pargeter's breeding and training establishment. To put it mildly, he was impressed. Green pastures. White stables. And everywhere he looked, expensive, beautifully cared for horseflesh. There was a wading pool where injured animals could be safely exercised and a completely equipped surgery where all but the most exotic treatments could be performed.

He found it easy to imagine himself working in these surroundings. And at various California tracks, too. For his duties, if he became Pargeter's full-time vet, would often take him to the races. But what he found impossible to visualize were his nonworking hours. Every time he tried, it was with Cassie that he pictured himself. Only Cassie wouldn't be there. Not in his arms, nor in his bed. Inside him was a hollow, a vacancy, where love and laughter once had lived, but now there was nothing but the ache of loss.

"That's about it, Doctor Faraday." Dan's thought were interrupted by the voice of the underling who had conducted the guided tour. The man gestured at the door of a small building near the main stable area. "Mr. Pargeter asked if you'd join him in the office after you'd seen around."

"Thanks," Dan said and knocked on the door.

Pargeter had greeted him cordially when he first arrived. Now he opened the door for Dan and smiled. "Well, what did you think?"

"I think it's a fantastic place. What a setup!"

"I'm rather proud of it," Pargeter admitted.

He showed Dan to a soft, suede-covered easy chair, then pressed a buzzer that summoned coffee. After it arrived, delivered by a sweet-faced Mexican woman Pargeter introduced as his housekeeper, he began to talk about horses. It took Dan a while to realize he was being subtly grilled. He didn't mind, but when nearly an hour had passed and Pargeter still hadn't said anything concrete about offering him a job, Dan began to feel uneasy. Maybe Pargeter was interviewing several vets. That was certainly the owner's right, but he would have expected the man to have said so, right up front.

Pargeter was saying, "Yes, I've always been partial to the Sassafras bloodlines. Speed, stamina and heart. You can't ask for more than that." He put his coffee cup down on the corner of his desk. "As a matter of fact, I've got a Sassafras colt in the barn right now that shows a lot of promise. Would you like to have a look?"

"I sure would."

Five minutes later, a groom led a high-strung chestnut into the yard. Dan verbally admired the beauty of the two-year-old. Pargeter nodded his head in the direction of the colt. "Go ahead. Check him over. I'd like to know what you think of his conditioning. He's running this Saturday."

Dan approached the horse slowly, murmuring, "Hello there, son. It's all right, fella." His experience had taught him that the main thing, with a nervous youngster, was to make no sudden moves . . . and to keep talking.

A few moments later, he frowned. Over his shoulder, his hand still touching one of the slender forelegs, he said to Pargeter, "You said this colt's running on Saturday? I don't think that's a very good idea."

"What?" Pargeter's scowl was instantaneous and ferocious. "Don't be ridiculous, Faraday. The colt's in great shape."

"No, I'm afraid he's not. There's heat in this leg. It could be a strained tendon."

Pargeter continued scowling. "He's got to run. He outclasses every other colt in the field. It's as sure a win as you can get in racing."

Dan's jaw tightened. Had he been wrong in thinking Pargeter put his horses' well-being above a single day's success? "A lame horse isn't going to run his best," he pointed out, trying to maintain a reasonable-sounding tone.

"It's simple then, isn't it? A little pain killer and the colt'll run just fine." Pargeter smiled ingratiatingly. "Who knows? You may be working for me by then. You could take care of it, couldn't you?"

"I could." He drew a deep breath, knowing he was throwing away this job with both hands. "But I wouldn't."

Pargeter's face got a black look. "Are you saying you wouldn't administer an injection, even if I ordered you to do it? I'm warning you, Faraday, I don't take kindly to insubordination."

"And I won't do anything, under any circumstances, that might endanger a horse." He pointed at the chestnut. "Run this colt anytime soon, and he could end up with a bowed tendon, damaged for life. Not to mention that what you're asking me to do is illegal." He sighed. "I guess I might as well go."

A smile blossomed unexpectedly on Pargeter's face. "It's a little soon for that, isn't it? We haven't had a chance to discuss your salary and benefits yet."

Dan couldn't believe what he was hearing. Seeing his stunned expression, Pargeter laughed. "You still haven't figured out that all that was just a little test? That colt isn't running this Saturday or any other Saturday until he's well."

Dan eyed Pargeter's smoothly shaven face. "You said you didn't believe the rumors that Winwood spread about me."

"I didn't."

"But you still felt that charade was necessary?" The word *charade* made him think of that evening at Cassie's house and then of Cassie, and he winced as the empty place inside him filled with pain.

"I'd have checked any vet the same way," Pargeter said carelessly. "Nothing personal, Faraday." He nodded toward the groom holding the colt's lead rope. "Put him back in his stall, Manuel. And get that cold pack back on his foreleg right away."

As the groom led the colt away, Pargeter clapped Dan on the shoulder. "Let's go back to my office. I'm about to make you an offer I hope you won't be able to refuse."

IT WAS LATE AFTERNOON. Feeding time. Cassie poured a measure of grain into Kettle's feed box. Eventually she'd get over losing Dan. She would become her old self again, finding contentment in the horses, her painting, her friends. But did she even *want* to revert to being the old Cassie? she wondered. She had tasted something different, better, more fulfilling . . . and she had thrown it away.

She shut Kettle's door, then turned down the aisle. Something made her glance into an empty stall, two down from Kettle's. A dark lumpy object caught her attention. It was in the very back, half-hidden in the straw. She hurried into the stall and stooped over. The object was a bundle wrapped up in a moth-eaten old blanket. Inside were several dirty articles of clothing, a pack of Camels, a half-used book of matches and a pony-sized bottle of cheap brandy.

Willie was back.

Ruthlessly, she took cigarettes, matches and bottle. After looking in the other empty stall and the tack room, she went outside the barn and shouted, "Willie!"

No reply. She raised her voice, yelling in the direction of the woods. "It's okay, Willie. You can sleep here tonight if you want. But no smoking and no drinking, okay?"

She hoped he was somewhere on the fringes of the woods where he could hear her. She doubted he would have gone far from his pitiful hoard of possessions. But there was no answer. She decided to leave the tack room door open for him. And a sandwich on a plate. Some hot coffee. It seemed only fair, since she'd stolen his brandy and cigarettes.

Somehow the evening passed. Several times she checked the barn for Willie. She never saw him, but once she went out and found the sandwich and the coffee gone. At her last check, his bundle of belongings was missing, too. She shouted for him, her voice caught and whipped away by the cold wind that blew around the barn. Still no answer, no sign of Willie anywhere. Evidently, having dined, he'd decided to sleep elsewhere tonight.

Between trips to the barn, Cassie kept thinking about priorities, about where love came on the list of what was important in her life. At first her thoughts surprised her, but then more and more they began to feel right. . . .

IF IT HADN'T BEEN for the ice on the winding road, Dan would have taken the highway up the mountain at breakneck speed—and probably would have gotten his neck broken as a consequence. It was just as well that he was forced to maintain a conservative pace. But the five-hour drive from Pargeter's place to Pinetop seemed to have lasted for days. An ox-drawn covered wagon could have made better time.

He could hardly wait to see Cassie. An hour or so ago, still down on the flatlands, he had decided that if it was necessary to wake her up, he would. He had to tell her what he had decided. No, not *decided*; what had happened to him in Pargeter's office was less a decision than a revelation.

Maybe half a mile to her place now. The car rounded a curve, and then he saw it. A red glow against the black sky. Fire! At Cassie's place or damn close to it.

A bare minute later, he brought the van to a screeching halt in the stable yard. It was the barn. The far end, the shed where she stored the hay, was ablaze. Tongues of flame shot into the sky. Over the crackling of the fire as it bit into dry hay and aged wood Dan could hear the screams of frightened horses. Cassie! Where was she? She couldn't be asleep with this racket going on.

Then he heard her voice from inside the barn. In there, in the smoke and heat, she was calling, "Willie! Willie! Where are you?"

Dan ran toward the open barn door. At half the distance, he saw something off to the right. It was Willie. The old man stumbled out of the woods, zipping up his fly. "Whatsa matter witha horses?" he asked drunkenly.

"Stay there! Keep away from the barn!" Dan ordered and plunged through the door.

Inside it wasn't quite as bad as he had feared. Only the shed was alight so far; the flames had not penetrated into the barn itself. Wisps of smoke, not the dense killing cloud he had dreaded, wafted down the wide central aisle.

His eyes adjusted to the dim light, and he saw Cassie near the middle of the barn, peering anxiously into a stall. Horses kicked wood, let out frightened whinnies. "Willie, where are you?" she yelled.

"He's outside," Dan shouted.

Her head whipped around. "Thank God! He must have decided to bunk in the shed. I took his cigarettes and matches, but he must have gotten more." She sagged for an instant in relief, then straightened. "We have to get the horses out."

She had left several of the stall doors open in her search for Willie. But somewhere back in time, the ancestors of the horse had acquired a paralyzing terror of fire. Not one animal had come out of his stall to save himself. All nine would have to be blindfolded and led away from the burning building. And unless they were taken a good distance away or confined some place safe, some might even, in their terror, plunge back into the burning building.

It was getting hotter in the barn. The far wall began to blacken, and one greedy flame got its finger through the wood.

Oh, God, Dan thought. There wouldn't be time to save them all.

"Blankets, halters. In the tack room," Cassie gasped. She ran past him and he followed her.

In the tack room she bundled towels, blankets, halters and lead ropes into his arms. Then, with a load of her own, she raced off down the barn's center aisle. His heart plummeted as he saw her heading toward the last stall, the one nearest the crackling tongues of flame that were greedily devouring the far wall.

Dan rushed to Kettle's stall. At least he could make sure that her favorite was rescued. Kettle reared and plunged as the stall door opened. His eyes were wild, rims of white showing the extent of the horse's panic. Dan took a second to immerse a towel in Kettle's water bowl. The litany came automatically. "Whoa there, son. Easy, son. Take it easy, fella."

Then, deftly avoiding the lethal front hooves, Dan tossed the wet towel over Kettle's head, praying it would stick. With the smell of fire muted by the covering, the animal calmed slightly, and Dan was able to buckle a halter around his neck. Tugging, still murmuring soothing words, he led Kettle out of the stall.

Cassie ran past him, leading a blindfolded horse. One of the boarders. Trust her to save other people's animals before her own. With her passing came a drift of smoke. The evil crackling of the flames was louder now.

No time. No time, Dan thought. The fire was taking hold too fast.

He got Kettle outside to see Cassie releasing the boarder's horse at the margin of the woods. Whipping the blanket she'd used as a blindfold from its head, she shouted, "Hyaw! Get on there!" and slapped the animal on the rump. It took off, galloping into the trees.

The corral was closer, and there the horses would be confined, but it wasn't safe, Dan realized. The fire might consume the entire barn, then leap to wooden fence rails when it needed more food.

He ran, leading Kettle, toward the woods. Why he noticed, he never knew, but something made him glance at Cassie's back porch. A dark man-sized shape lay near the door. Willie, passed out. Probably the old man had no idea what he had done.

Cassie came running back toward Dan. "Be careful!" he said sharply. His heart felt huge with fear for her. What if he lost her now, just when everything was going to be all right? He couldn't bear the thought of it.

"Keep a wet towel with you," he shouted. "If the smoke..." He meant to tell her that if the smoke started getting to her, she should cover her mouth and nose and crawl out, below smoke level.

"I know, Dan," she said. She ran on into the barn.

He turned Kettle loose at the edge of the woods, then raced back. Only two saved. Seven to go. And the fire now had the barn's entire far end in its maw. Flames shot up the wall and eddied along the roof. When they had eaten through, the roof would collapse. The horses left inside would die in terror. How many would they have time to save? Two more? Four? How many would be left to die?

He dashed to the barn. He was just inside the barn door, intending to go to the end where Cassie was. He meant to stick close, to watch and make certain she was safe. With the flames roaring, the horses screaming and kicking, he almost didn't hear it. But something made him turn his head and look outside. He saw the twin lights of a car pulling into the yard. Behind it, another and another. More cars were coming down the road. And from somewhere, not too far away, he heard the siren on the truck owned by the town's volunteer fire department.

Cars stopped. Doors opened. Coated and gloved figures scrambled out, calling above the crackle of the flames.

The people of Pinetop had come to help their neighbor.

WITH A BLANKET DRAPED around her shoulders, Cassie sat at her kitchen table. Her face felt greasy with soot, and her hands stung where sparks had burned them. Half her barn and most of its roof was sodden ash and charred timbers. But she didn't care. The horses were all safe in the corral.

After the fire was out, her friends and neighbors had gone into the woods, armed with flashlights, to round up the animals. Every one had been found. Dan had checked them briefly. No major injuries, he had reported. A few coats were singed, a few legs scraped, but there was nothing requiring immediate treatment.

Willie had been collected from the front porch and was spending the night in jail, although not as a prisoner. Something would have to be done about Willie, a way found to help the pitiful old man. Cassie was confident that the people of the town, working together, would be able to come up with a solution.

She sighed and looked across the table at Dan. His face was streaked with black, his eyes red-rimmed from the smoke. His hands, like hers, were marked by tiny burns. He had never looked worse, and she had never loved him more.

She wondered if this was the right time to tell him what she had decided. He looked so worn out. And yet, what better time than now, after what they had been through together?

She wrapped her stinging hands around her coffee cup and said, "Dan, there's something I have to tell you."

He looked up at her. A half smile tilted his mouth. "Funny. There's something I need to say, too."

She gave a little shake of her head. "Me first. I'll keep it simple. If you still want me to go with you when you leave Pinetop, I will."

"Because of what happened tonight?" He leaned across the table and gently touched the back of her hand, seeking an unburned spot so he wouldn't hurt her. "You can rebuild the barn, you know. You're insured, aren't you?"

"Of course." For a brief instant, she feared that he no longer wanted her to live with him. But she realized he wouldn't want her to come with him only because of the fire.

"That has nothing to do with it," she said. "Actually I'd made up my mind before the fire started. I've done a lot of thinking, the past couple of days. I love this place, these people. You know that. But I love you more. It's that simple, Dan."

A slow smile spread across his face; delight sparkled in his eyes. "Well, how about that?" The look he gave her was filled with love. "Come on over here, honey. You're too far away."

She rose, letting the blanket fall from her shoulders and rushed around the table to be close to him. He pulled her down onto his lap and pressed a kiss onto her sweaty, sooty forehead, then said, "You said that you loved this place, these people."

"But I love you more," she repeated, wanting to reassure him that her willingness to go with him was for the right reasons.

"And I love you, too. With all my heart." He tightened his grip on her. "The point is, you can have both. I've decided to stay in Pinetop. Doc Anderson's offered to let me buy his practice. I turned him down before, but—"

"I know," Cassie interrupted. "I heard about it a while back."

"You did? You never said anything."

"Neither did you."

"I know." He grimaced. "I felt guilty about not telling you, but I just didn't want to bring up a potentially unpleasant subject."

"Me, either." Her initial joy at Dan's announcement was now laced with misgivings. How happy would he be if he viewed his life here as defeat—second best, because he couldn't have what he really wanted? "I guess," she said slowly, not wanting to hurt, "that your trip today must not have worked out the way you hoped."

Dan grinned. "You're wrong. Pargeter offered me the job."

"I didn't mean that," Cassie said loyally. "I knew he'd offer it to you. He'd have had to be crazy not to. I was just guessing that you must have decided the working conditions weren't what you wanted."

"That's not it, either," Dan said. "The place was fantastic. An equine vet's dream."

She glared at him accusingly, which was difficult with their faces so close together. "Why are we playing guessing games?"

"Because it's fun," Dan suggested. That was one of the things he had long since realized—that life with Cassie would be fun. A lot of other things, too, of course.

She rapped him on the chest with her knuckles. "Enough fun. Start explaining, mister."

He shifted position, so that one of his arms grazed the side of her breast. His body's predictable response made him decide to keep his explanation brief. "I discovered today that it was terribly important to me to be offered a job in racing."

Cassie inhaled sharply. "And you still turned it down? Because of me? Oh, Dan, I hope you don't regret it one day." A terrible question occurred to her: What if, in the dark moments that all loves must endure, he blamed her for what he'd given up?

"You're not paying attention," he said severely. "I said it was important to me to be *offered* a job. As vindication, I guess. Proof—to myself, at least—that I could go back to racing if I wanted to." A grin played around the corners of his eyes. "But the funniest thing happened. The minute Pargeter mentioned salary—quite a decent salary, by the way—I realized that the offer itself was all I needed. That as far as the actual work went, I'd be happier here."

It hadn't hurt a bit that Pargeter had confided to Dan that the HBPA planned to call Owen Winwood on the carpet sometime during the next week or two. There was every likelihood that Winwood would be banned from racing for a long time.

Cassie inhaled sharply. He really meant it. Being here wouldn't be second best. It was all she could have asked for, all she'd ever dreamed of.

He grinned at her. "I guess I've gotten hooked on dogs and cats. I could still skip the pig, though."

It had also occurred to him—finally—that he didn't have to be a racetrack vet to make good use of his training in equine medicine. It would require building a special surgical facility for horses; it would take time for his reputation to spread. But it could be done. It was something to discuss with Cassie. There was no hurry, though. There would be plenty of time for that discussion, and many others, over the years.

Cassie rubbed her sooty cheek against his equally grimy one. "Admit it, Dan Faraday, you've also gotten hooked on Pinetop."

"That's true, too." When he had seen those people—half the town, at least—driving into Cassie's yard, he had realized something fundamental about this place, and why she was so attached to it. "The main thing is that I'm hooked on you. I want you to marry me, Cassie. Right away."

A bubble of joy swelled inside her. She hung on tighter to Dan, as if, without him as an anchor, she might float up to the ceiling. Happiness acted as a balm, she discovered. The stinging in her hands was gone. But new sensations were creeping in. Familiar quivers and flutters. She couldn't be feeling desire for him *now*, she thought. Not after the exhausting terrifying events they'd been through. But there were those familiar, cherished sensations. A stirring beneath her, in Dan's lap, proved that she wasn't the only one whose body was reacting to their proximity.

"Getting married sounds like a good idea," she said, then paused, a slight frown forming between her brows. "Wait a minute! Shouldn't we live together for a while first, to see if it works out? I mean, that's what most people do these days, isn't it?"

Dan nuzzled her ear. "I don't see any reason why we need to. We've been virtually living together for the last month anyway."

"I guess you're right."

"We'll have a lot to do," Dan warned her. "We might have to postpone the honeymoon for a while. I'll have to arrange with Doc Anderson to buy the practice. And there'll be the fire insurance to deal with and builders and . . ."

"Can't we talk about all that tomorrow?" Cassie complained. "I want a shower."

"Is that all you want?" he teased. He looked at the front of her. The hardening of her nipples was evident beneath her shirt. The ache in his own groin was becoming more acute. He *had* to make love to her tonight. It would be like the very first time. And, in a way, it *would* be a first time. The first time they could both be sure of "forever."

"Nope." She looked at him—her red-eyed, sooty-faced Prince Charming—and her heart ached with love. She could see the years marching forward. Their life in Pinetop, their children growing. She could even imagine a time when he would be "good old Doc Faraday" and she, perhaps, "that wacky old wife of his who runs the livery stable and paints them crazy pictures."

That was what she wanted. All of it. And all the in-between years, too.

She grinned impishly and said, "You'll find out what I want, Doc." Then she leaped off his lap. "Last one in the shower's a rotten egg."

COMING NEXT MONTH

#261 SOPHISTICATED LADY
Candace Schuler

As the model for an exclusive line of cosmetics, Samantha
Spencer wasn't so much attracted by fame and fortune as
she was by Alex Gavino's old-world charm. She knew he'd
hired her for her cool, sophisticated looks, unaware of the
fire under the ice. But once she took the wraps off, he'd
know what passion was all about....

#262 A STROKE OF GENIUS Gina Wilkins

Mallory Littlefield's gorgeous new boss, Elliott Frazer, was a
certified genius. But the poor man was completely
incompetent when it came to day-to-day life. Free-spirited
Mallory was soon teaching him everything she knew—from
driving a car to dancing. And it didn't take a high IQ to
guess where the lessons were leading.

#263 WHEN FORTUNE SMILES
Sally Bradford

When yuppie dentist Alex Carson invaded Gretchen
Bauer's apartment, lock, stock and jock equipment,
Gretchen became suspicious. She was in dire financial need,
so any roommate—male or female—was a godsend. But
Alex didn't have to count pennies. If he was planning to
share more than the rent, her home would soon be
transformed into a battleground...or a love nest....

#264 AN UNMARRIED MAN
Sarah Hawkes

Alec Lindfors thought posing as a married man would save
him from commitment-seeking women. But after meeting
Michelle, he didn't know if he *wanted* to be saved. Nor did
he know she was on to his little deception....

Harlequin American Romance®

Gull Cottage

The sun, the surf, the sand...

One relaxing month by the sea was all Zoe,
Diana and Gracie ever expected from their
four-week stay at Gull Cottage, the luxurious
East Hampton mansion. They never thought
that what they found at the beach would
change their lives forever.

Join Zoe, Diana and Gracie for the summer of
their lives. Don't miss the GULL COTTAGE
trilogy in Harlequin American Romance: #301
CHARMED CIRCLE by Robin Francis (July
1989); #305 MOTHER KNOWS BEST by
Barbara Bretton (August 1989); and #309
SAVING GRACE by Anne McAllister
(September 1989).

GULL COTTAGE—because one month can be
the start of forever...

Have You Ever Wondered If You Could Write A Harlequin Novel?

Here's great news—Harlequin is offering a series of cassette tapes to help you do just that. Written by Harlequin editors, these tapes give practical advice on how to make your characters—and your story—come alive. There's a tape for each contemporary romance series Harlequin publishes.

Mail order only

All sales final

TO: **Harlequin Reader Service**
Audiocassette Tape Offer
P.O. Box 1396
Buffalo, NY 14269-1396

I enclose a check/money order payable to HARLEQUIN READER SERVICE® for $9.70 ($8.95 plus 75¢ postage and handling) for EACH tape ordered for the total sum of $_____*
Please send:

☐ Romance and Presents   ☐ Intrigue
☐ American Romance   ☐ Temptation
☐ Superromance   ☐ All five tapes ($38.80 total)

Signature_____
                                             (please print clearly)
Name:_____
Address:_____
State:_____ Zip:_____

*Iowa and New York residents add appropriate sales tax.

AUDIO-H